BLOOD JAGUAR

ALLAN SERAFINO

This is a work of fiction. Names, characters, places and incidents are either the product of the author's imagination or are used fictitiously, and any resemblance to any person or persons, living or dead, events, or locales is entirely coincidental.

Blood Jaguar by Allan Serafino
ISBN 1-55316-570-5
Published by LTDBooks
www.ltdbooks.com

Published in Canada by LTDBooks, 200 North Service Road West, Unit 1, Suite 301, Oakville, ON L6M 2Y1

Printed in Canada.

National Library of Canada Cataloguing in Publication Data

Serafino, Allan
Blood jaguar

ISBN 1-55316-570-5

I. Title.

PS8587.E7B56 2003 C813'.54 C2002-905747-7
PR9199.3.S444B56 2003

For Maureen

Thanks also to the Kensington Writers Group.

CHAPTER 1

The spotted jaguar paced back and forth inside the cage, powerful muscles rippling under its glossy coat. It slammed its body against the bars at each turn and then, raising its sleek head, let out a piercing scream through fanged teeth.

In the noisy *zocalo*, only Hugh Falkins seemed to hear the cry. It sent an icy shiver along the hairs on his neck but the hundreds of buyers and sellers crammed in the busy Mexican plaza went on with their daily business.

Hugh locked eyes with the jaguar. As he gazed into its golden eyes, he sensed the cat's fear and frustration and for a moment he was one with the animal, inside its body and mind. He moved across the distance between them as if in a dream, and reached out to touch it.

"No tengo!"

A stick slashed across his hand. Hugh yelled in pain and snatched back his hand.

"Stupid American. You want to get killed?" the cat's owner shouted.

"I just wanted to touch—"

"No! No touch!" The man raised the stick again.

It never fell. A uniformed man forced his way between them. "Leave the boy alone," he commanded. "He's with me."

The seller's eyes smoldered but he lowered the stick, backing away with an angry gesture.

"Come away from there, Senor Falkins." Hugh's rescuer tugged at his sleeve.

Hugh recognized his white uniform with the stylized *S* insignia of Sheldon Enterprises. The man was barely five feet tall. He had dark olive-colored skin, a hooked nose and black curly hair. He shook hands with Hugh.

"Thanks," Hugh said. "You must be Senor Dario."

"Si. I have come to get you. I have your letter saying you arrive from Florida."

The jaguar coughed, a sound like the low rumble of thunder.

"Why is he caged? He shouldn't be trapped like that."

The pilot shrugged. "He will bring a good price."

The cat's eyes connected again with Hugh's. It thrust its paws between the bars as if reaching out to him but the grumbling seller snapped the stick across them with a resounding crack. The jaguar recoiled with a sharp yowl and threw itself against the bars until the seller finally threw a dark blanket over the cage to silence the animal. He turned on the pilot in a spate of anger.

"He says don't be sorry," Dario said. "The animal is *muy demente. Loco.* And very dangerous. Already it has hurt one man. Don't waste your time on it. The jeep is that way." Dario led him toward the far end of the plaza.

"I pick up supplies for the camp first. That is why I ask to meet you here and not the airport. It will take us one hour to fly you to Yaxchilán."

Yaxchilán. The ancient Mayan archaeological site where his father was now working was like a dream to Hugh. All his careful planning would take him there soon if something didn't go wrong. He was anxious and nervous even though, at sixteen, he had traveled to foreign countries before. But this was his first visit to southern Mexico. And the first time he was alone.

He carried only one light packsack, yet it was hard to keep up with the small man as they pushed their way through the crowd. At four o'clock in the afternoon, the market square was noisy and full of strange smells and exotic sights. Hugh wanted to see everything but Dario strode past the women dressed in white embroidered *huipiles* who called out their wares for sale: "peppers, beans, squash, corn!" They displayed stalls of fresh bananas, pineapples and melons. He wrinkled his nose as they passed chickens clucking in basket cages, butchered pigs hanging from the braces of awnings, and caged ducks and rabbits and monkeys lining the walkways. The smells of overripe fruit, spices and the hot-griddle aroma of *tortillas* jangled his taste buds. His last meal had been on the plane that morning.

In an adjoining area under tents, men hawked clothes and archaeological artifacts—terracotta figurines, potsherds and jade carvings—and he recalled his father's bristling anger at the illicit trade in ancient carvings stolen from archaeological digs. "They'll ruin everything for those of us who really care," he had often complained.

A vendor wearing a stack of straw hats stepped in front of Hugh, blocking his way. *"Sombrero,* Senor*? Mas barato."*

Dario turned to look at Hugh thoughtfully. "You have no hat?" he asked.

"I didn't bring one." In his hurry to get away, he hadn't packed any clothes for the hot Mexican climate.

"You must," Dario insisted. "It is very hot in the jungle where you are going. He says these are cheap. Let me bargain for you." He paid for a wide-brimmed sisal hat that Hugh slanted over his long blond hair.

Checking his reflection in a mirror the seller held out to him, he laughed nervously. "Hey! This is great. Indiana Falkins! If only my friends could see me now."

The jeep, already loaded down with boxes of supplies for the camp, looked like an over-packed donkey where it crouched in the shade of a tree. It groaned and belched black smoke when Dario put the key in the ignition. Soon they were out of the busy commercial area and on their way. Hugh was glad to feel the cool breeze on his skin after the close humidity of the marketplace. They veered off the main road toward a local airfield where a Cessna single-engine plane awaited them. There, they transferred the boxes containing everything from medicines to groceries. They strapped them in and were ready to go.

Dario revved the engine. "Soon you will see your father," he yelled above the noise.

Hugh took a deep breath as the runway slid away beneath them. Relax, he told himself. This is it. End of the road. He is my father. He has to take me. Hugh hoped he had made the right decision in running away from home.

"I'm going to marry Sam Sheldon!"

That's the way it had started. A bolt out of the blue. But, no, he had seen the signs of his parents' break-up earlier than that.

"The field trip is only for two months, Eve. Why won't you come? You always have before."

Hugh could hear his father's voice through the thin bedroom wall. He shouldn't have been listening, but…

"You and Sheldon. That's it, isn't it?"

"Roger, I'm tired of living in dirt camps. Sure, it was fun in the beginning, but now I'm tired and I have my own career…"

"And what about Hugh? We're a team. We have been for years."

"He's got to think about his school. He's got his own life to think about."

"And Sheldon can..."

Hugh had heard no more. He crumbled inside. His fault. His fault. If it weren't for him, they would still be a team, traveling around the world. As for Sheldon, he didn't dislike the man exactly, but the entrepreneur was too reserved for him. Hugh was extra baggage.

The sound of the plane's engine made him sleepy.

His mother saw in Sheldon those things she never had with his father: security, comfort and normalcy. Hugh loved his father for not being "normal"—he was exciting. He would think nothing of suddenly dragging his family to the far corners of the world. And Hugh missed him with a mixture of bitterness and despair that he found overwhelming. But his father had also deserted him, and the knowledge hurt every time he remembered. Now, all he had of his father was the ring. He turned it on his finger so the carving of the silver falcon, the family crest that was hundreds of years old, glimmered with intensity in the light coming through the window.

The plane leveled out as Dario maneuvered the joystick and rudder pedals, trimming the balance with practised ease. He called out to Hugh as the engine's noise settled to a regular hum. "He is happy to see you? Your father?"

"Yeah, I guess he'll be happy to see me. I mean, it's going to be a surprise."

"It is good for a son to be with his father. My children, I have three." He held up his fingers to show Hugh. "The Senor Falkins, he don't talk about you. I don't know he has a son."

Hugh pretended not to hear him and looked away.

The plane slid easily through the air, and the cityscape, lit with the dull orange glow of refinery fires, disappeared behind them. They were leaving the rich oil country of the Mexican gulf for the mysterious green interior of the jungle.

Within minutes they were flying over the river.

Dario pointed below. "Usumascinta. The site is right beside the river. About thirty minutes."

The river was a delta of muddy streams that became a single, twisting snake through the jungle as they flew onward. Its cliffs were high and steep and, at points, Hugh saw the telltale flash of rapids. It was not a place where he would likely make use of his newly learned scuba diving skills.

The jungle below tugged at his memory. It looked oddly familiar, yet that couldn't be. He'd never been in a Mexican jungle before. He became aware of voices, muffled, rising in an eerie chant. He couldn't make out what they were saying over the pounding drums. He pressed his hands to his temples for the sounds were coming from *inside* his head. His vision blurred as if he were stepping through a heavy mist, and ghostly figures swam before his eyes, causing him to become nauseous. He fell forward, his head spinning.

"Senor! Senor! Are you all right?" Dario shook him with his free hand, his face etched with concern. "Are you sick?"

"No. No, I'm fine." Hugh shook his head and the voices stopped. The ghosts disappeared as if they'd never been. "Just the heat, I guess."

"You must try to take it easy. It is very hot in the afternoon." Dario motioned to a cooler behind him. "Have a *Coca*."

Hugh pulled a bottle of cola for each of them. The sharp taste soothed his jangled nerves and he began to wonder if it wasn't just the heat after all. Even in the cockpit, he could feel humidity rising from the jungle below. He'd probably fallen asleep and dreamed the whole thing. Yet the incident had been disturbing—even a little frightening.

"Will my father be at the camp?"

"The *professores* are out at the digging. But they all come back soon. The jungle is no place to be alone at night."

"I hope they can use an extra hand."

"Hand?" Dario looked confused.

"Me. An extra worker."

Dario seemed to find this amusing. "Ah, yes, I think so. But you may not want to stay, my young friend." He didn't wait for Hugh to inquire but went on. "That place is bad luck. All the time, things are going wrong."

"What things?"

"Many accidents with the work. Some men are getting sick. One, he has the snakebite. Very dangerous the snakes. Another is hurt with the *machete*."

"Oh!" Hugh gulped.

"Si. Very bad."

"Is it safe?"

"I would be careful."

The green jungle floated beneath them, placid and quiet, and even when they passed over the river village Dario called Frontera Echeverria, he saw only an empty river outpost.

Dario pulled a packet of cigarettes from his breast pocket and offered one to Hugh.

Hugh shook his head, waiting to hear more.

The pilot tapped out a cigarette and proceeded to light it. He slowly blew a plume of smoke from his lungs and continued.

"But still they don't find the thing they look for. Many days have passed with much worry. And now the Senor Sheldon is unhappy too. He comes to see in a few days."

Hugh jolted upright. "What? You mean Sheldon is coming to the camp?"

"Si, the big man, my boss. Samuel Sheldon. He comes. He does not like, I think, to spend his money for to find nothing, no?"

"No, he wouldn't," Hugh agreed. He turned his face back to the window again, pretending interest in the scenery below, trying not to give away the worry on his face. Damn! Sheldon coming to the site? He'd be caught for sure. What if Sheldon had already figured out Hugh's trick and radioed ahead to the camp? What if Dario already knew? What if his father were waiting?

A bead of perspiration trickled down his neck like a hot ember.

Sheldon. Coming to Yaxchilán. Hugh saw his carefully laid out plan falling apart like a house of cards. In the beginning, he had needed to find out exactly where his father was. As his birthday was approaching, he had asked his mother, as a present, to visit his father. She had rounded on him sharply. "I don't know where he is and I don't want to know. Ask Sam if you're that interested."

He asked one of his father's colleagues instead.

"Yaxchilán," David Cameron sighed. He pronounced it Yash-she-lan. "Middle of the Chiapas jungle in central Mexico. Site of one of the most important Mayan cities. And now your father's got Sheldon's money, so he'll be sitting pretty down there, too. No financial worries. Sheldon goes down in his own private plane, I understand." He raised a hopeful eyebrow but Hugh was already lost in thought. He'd figured out how to use Sheldon's influence to get him to Mexico.

He stole a piece of Sheldon Enterprises letterhead and wrote to the company office, asking for a pilot to pick him up in Villahermosa, the nearest big city to the site. He forged Sheldon's signature. After that, he bought an airline ticket from Tampa to Villahermosa with his college savings. Hugh shook all the way to the airport that day but it was too late to reconsider now.

In what he hoped was a relaxed voice, he asked Dario, "What are they looking for down there?"

The pilot shrugged. "Temples, ruins. They all want the treasure of Los Mayas."

"Have they found any?" Hugh's pulse began to quicken.

Dario laughed. "You too, I see. The blood, it goes fast, heh? The eyes glaze. Everyone wants gold. But I tell you, the old ones do not give up their secrets. You must be careful down there."

"I just want to see my father."

"Then I hope it will go well. I tell you, my young friend, that is not a happy place to be. I don't stay there—I go back as fast as I can. See your father but leave quick too."

Hugh stared down at the canopy of green. He'd come too far to leave now. And Sheldon or no Sheldon, he'd make his stand.

Their flight path took them directly upriver to the site of the ancient Mayan ruins. "We arrive," Dario shouted and gave the engine more revs.

As they dropped into the river canyon, the jungle canopy came up at them like a green fist. Hugh barely had time to make out a short, narrow airstrip etched on the deep canyon terrace on the west side and the flashing white of ancient stone buildings thrusting up out of the forest as they roared by on the test run.

Dario banked the plane in a wide curve and prepared for his final approach. "Over there," he indicated the left side, "Guatemala border. We don't go too close. They shoot at us."

The engine roared. Dario throttled back and lowered the flaps. Using the landmark cliffs on the Guatemalan side, he took them down from a thousand feet in a stomach-curdling drop and leveled out just above the water. Waves flashed by as Hugh was thrust forward against his seat belt.

They nosed down, this time in a gradual and controlled descent. Hugh got a better glimpse of the Mayan ruins almost hidden in the foliage—the top of a crumbled white pyramid. He saw a huge white temple with broad steps leading down to the waterside. He saw—he thought he saw—hundreds of people lining the steps. There was a sudden, blinding flash…red blood…A stab of pain shot through his side as if he'd been stabbed and he cried out.

Dario lost control—just for a second—but the plane rocked sharply as the winds from the river punched against the undercarriage. The airstrip loomed before them and the plane slammed onto the beaten path.

They plunged toward a wall of trees.

Hugh was thrown forward against the restraining belt and back again into the seat. His chest exploded with pain and his head whirled in a shower of lights.

Dario yanked back on the throttle with all his might. The plane hammered on the ground and spun to the right, careening wildly, but he jerked the wheel left and they shuddered down the narrow runway, stopping short of a massive tree trunk.

Hugh gasped for air, his chest jerking in spasms.

The tide of pain finally gave way and he turned to Dario who was slumped over the controls. Hugh thought the man had been hurt but the pilot sat up groggily then, his breath rasping, and Hugh realized he had been holding his own too. He let it out, thankful that the pilot's natural instincts and training had taken over quickly.

Dario sat up and switched off the engine. He reached for a crucifix on a chain around his neck and kissed it fervently. Then he looked at Hugh. "What happened? You yell out just as we land."

"Sorry. Something just came over me. I got scared all of a sudden. I don't know why." His pulse was still racing.

Dario mopped his brow with a handkerchief. "Here is very tricky to land. But we are safe. *Gracias a Dios.*"

Thanks be to God and thanks to you too, Hugh said to himself. What a way to make his arrival!

The door on Hugh's side was tugged opened. "Holy cow, you guys all right?" A redheaded boy about his own age peered in.

Dario undid his seat belt and motioned to Hugh to do the same. "We're fine, Mitch. Just a little trouble on the landing."

"A little trouble? I thought you were gonna be mashed potatoes. What happened?"

Dario caught Hugh's glance and winked. "A sudden cross-current. Nothing serious."

Hugh slid down to the ground. His legs were shaky and he was still dizzy. He had no rational explanation for the flash of light and the sudden jab of pain.

"Hey, Dario, I thought you weren't due for another few days," Mitch said.

The pilot shrugged and closed the door. "Ask him. Special delivery from Senor Sheldon himself."

Mitch looked Hugh square in the face, removing the wide hat to wipe away a line of sweat.

Surprised, Hugh saw that Mitch was really a girl, about sixteen, her face well tanned. Her reddish hair, cut short, emphasized her boyish features.

She rammed her hat back on her head, glaring at Hugh. "Who are you?"

"I'm Hugh Falkins. My father—"

"The head honcho's son, huh? Didn't know he had one. Well, nobody asked me to get ready for another mouth to feed. What am I supposed to do with you? Hey, Dario." She turned to the pilot who was shouldering a heavy box. "You got my tapes?"

"Si, Senorita—Rolling Stones, Crashing Porcupines. The best."

"Smashing Pumpkins, you mean. Aw-rrright!" She leaned into the plane's cargo hold and pulled down a heavy bundle with ease.

Hugh joined in the unloading. In minutes, the boxes were piled on the ground.

Mitch, whose face was hidden under the brim of her wide hat, worked quickly and efficiently. When she finished, she hefted two bags onto her shoulders and headed inland, following Dario.

Hugh didn't want to be left behind. Grabbing a couple of bags, he started after them.

They worked their way up a steep, well-worn path. Sweat trickled into his eyes and soaked his shirt. His breath came in short gasps as he stumbled along behind them. The other two seemed not to be bothered by the steepness of the climb at all. Soon they broke into a clearing in the jungle. He'd been aware of the jungle as a dark background around him but now he could see that the white-barked trees rose like thick legs thirty to forty feet above him, and their green foliage nearly closed off the sky.

There were no temples. Instead, the clearing was dominated by tents, thatched wooden buildings, and a few more enclosures made of stone and roofed with coppery, galvanized tin.

They dumped their loads on long picnic tables under a wide awning and headed back to the plane. Hugh followed, though after two more trips, he was sweating profusely. The humidity was oppressive, sucking all the strength from his body. He slumped onto one of the tables and fanned himself with his hat.

There was no one else about—no reception committee, other than the girl. Hadn't anyone else heard the plane? Then he remembered Dario saying they were all at work deep in the jungle.

He gazed disconsolately at his surroundings.

"Kitchen tent there." Mitch inclined her head. "That's the lab and the collections building; the thatched huts are for storage and the permanent ones are showers. Toilet's just up the trail. This here's the mess hall. We call it the lunchroom. Kind of reminds you of school, doesn't it?"

"Yes, but with ants." Hugh pointed to a long line of the insects crawling along the table.

"You get used to them. Look, we'll finish unloading the rest of the plane, okay? You look pretty whacked, so you stay here. It's cooler."

"Sure," he agreed. Sure, the steep climb had tired him but why was the girl able to do more work than him? And without effort?

It was just after five o'clock and the sun was going down behind the steep western slope. The place was quiet except for the occasional squawk of birds high up in the trees and the faint rustling of leaves caused by a breeze.

He yawned. He'd been traveling for sixteen hours, from Tampa, Florida, across the Gulf of Mexico to Merida on the Yucatán peninsula, southwest to Villahermosa and then to Yaxchilán. He was hungry and so tired he could have fallen asleep at the table. But he wandered around the campsite to satisfy his curiosity.

Archaeological digs weren't new to him so he wasn't surprised at the rough living arrangements. The showers were in simple concrete buildings; water provided by a large rain cistern on the roof and shuttled through a pipe to a nozzle. A wooden shack housed the toilets—the hole-in-a-wooden-seat variety with a removable can underneath. Hugh laughed at the sign on the door crudely marked "Relax-Inn."

The lab was more interesting. Collapsible tables like those in the lunchroom were littered with archaeological paraphernalia: reference books, maps with grids marking out the ruins, boxes of potsherds and plastic artifact bags.

He stopped abruptly.

A skeleton lay on the table.

CHAPTER 2

The hairs rose on the nape of Hugh's neck. He shivered. Then he saw that the skeleton was an archaeological artifact. He laughed nervously and, drawing in a deep breath, crept forward. The bones were encrusted in dirt and labeled with small cards. He read one tied to an arm. *Humerus. Left. Female. Homo sapiens. Circa 700 AD.* There was an archaeological plot number as well. Beside the skull lay a jade necklace, dulled by the passage of time, yet tantalizing in its richness. The image of a woman in a white robe shimmered before his eyes.

"She's a beauty, isn't she?"

Hugh yelped in surprise and spun around.

A short, robust man stood in the doorway. He wore a khaki shirt and shorts and he took off a sisal hat to reveal a well-lined, sunburned face and thin reddish hair. He chuckled in a deep, gravelly voice. "Didn't mean to scare you. Heard the plane come in. Matthew McVean." He held out a large, rough hand.

"Hi. I'm Hugh Falkins."

The man's eyes widened. "Well, well...This is unexpected."

"Uh, yeah. Kind of a surprise visit. What about the skeleton?"

McVean gave a low burbling laugh. "Oh, Lady. Amazing find. We don't know who she is but she's likely the wife of a nobleman of the seventh or eighth century, maybe even the wife of the king."

"Shield Jaguar."

"Perhaps. Or his son, Bird Jaguar. You've done your homework, I see. Should have expected it from an archaeologist's son." He picked up the jade necklace. "This was around her neck when we found her. Now, you don't get one of these if you're just the hired help. It's a mark of nobility. Yet there's no other jewelry in her burial plot and no hieroglyphs giving a clue to her name, which should be the case with most noble people. She seems to have been laid out quickly and crudely."

McVean held the necklace lovingly. "Since we don't know her name, we call her *The Mysterious Lady*. Lady, for short. Go ahead. Touch her if you'd like."

Hugh caressed her, aware that he was touching a human being twelve hundred years old. She gave off a warm radiance and he found himself holding his breath as if the bones or the spirit of Lady might tell him her ancient secret. He heard voices, soft and distant.

"She's beautiful," he said, gently laying the bone back on the table. "By the way, is my dad here?"

McVean shrugged. "Haven't seen him all day." He stepped over to a refrigerator. "I just came for these." He pulled out two canisters of film.

Hugh was intrigued to see the refrigerator was filled with bones and artifacts as well as several bottles of soda.

"Look," McVean said, "I've gotta go, so if I see your father, I'll tell him you're here. But don't worry, we'll all be back by seven. Help yourself to some pop. Mitch will fix you up with anything else you need."

"Funny name for a girl."

"Michelle, actually. My daughter."

Hugh saw the resemblance then, especially the red hair.

He must have frowned for McVean chuckled. "I see you've met her. Bit short on social skills, that girl. My fault, I suppose. But hey, don't let her get to you. Her bark's worse than her bite." He paused. "She's our logistical technician—that is, she's the general camp organizer and dogsbody, and cook too, ever since our hired woman ran off because of the ghosts. Anyway, ask Mitch to find you a bed somewhere in this mess." He waved good-bye and left.

Hugh wasn't thinking about Mitch. Had McVean said ghosts? The brief image of Lady shimmered through his thoughts again.

As Mitch returned with the last of the supplies, the Cessna roared overhead on its way back to Villahermosa. Then the noise was gone and the camp was quiet again.

Mitch began to sort through the boxes and cases.

"Can I help with that?" he asked.

She tossed him a cursory glance. "You'll just get in the way."

"Mitch. That's an odd name. I like Michelle better."

"Who told you that?"

"Your father. He was here a moment ago."

"Well, don't call me that. It's Mitch."

Hugh tossed his hat on the table. "Okay. And don't call me Bones."

She snickered. "Bones? Really?"

"Yeah. It's what the guys at school call me. When you've got an archaeologist for a father, you have to put up with a lot of crap."

She picked up his packsack and tossed it to him. "You'll need a place to stay. I suppose you're staying? Take that tent over there."

Hugh was relieved. At least she had been civil. The tent contained two camp tables but no bed. He hung his pack on a hook and went back out.

Mitch grudgingly accepted Hugh's help in making supper. He asked her whether Dario's stories about trouble at the camp were true.

Ripping open a sack of potatoes, Mitch threw a dozen of them into a large pot and slammed the lid. "We haven't got troubles, mister, we've got a class one disaster. Our surveyor got bitten by a snake, the generator's on the fritz, the ants got into the sugar and the ghosts are scaring the pants off the workers."

"Ghosts?"

"The ghosts of Mayan slaves who built the old sites. They come out at night and start jabbering away like crazy. Creepy. And then everyone's so ticked off at each other," she continued, "it's a wonder they're not tearing out each other's throats. You've come at a bad time, that's for sure."

"But you've just found a whole skeleton with a jade necklace. That's wonderful."

Mitch twisted the loose flaps of the potato sack as if she was throttling someone's neck. She glared at him. "Wonderful? Yeah, for your old man. He'll get credit for the find, him and his mystical mumbo-jumbo. He's got the most incredible luck I've seen in a million years, and right under the nose of his pompous highness, Dr. Hartmann Schele, whose nose is so badly out of joint for not finding it himself, it's pointing backward. Not that my dad's any happier for it either. He's head of excavations and his team should have found it but didn't. They're mighty put out by your famous father, that's for sure."

"Well, I've come to help my father. We've worked together before."

"Oh, really?" Mitch heaved the heavy sack onto a shelf as if it had little weight. "I suppose you get dreams too?"

"What do you mean?"

"Like I said, he dreams where old things are buried. But," she pointed out, "he can't find the boy-king. And that means trouble for all of us. If we don't find him soon it could be the end of the project."

A sudden torrent of rain drowned out further conversation. There was no warning—one moment the sun was shining, next, the skies opened. They rushed to get the remaining supplies under cover of the lunchroom awning but were soaked before they could finish. The rain didn't bother Mitch. "Take a *siesta*," she yelled. "I am." With that, she clamped her hat on her head, and disappeared into the rain.

Hugh felt the weight of fatigue and confusion overpower him. As he watched the rain turn the dry baked compound to a soggy mess, he realized that he'd been stressed by the odd behavior of his new acquaintances. He was also troubled by the strange voices and images he had heard. Or dreamed. He decided rest was the best cure after all.

Shoving together the two rickety tables in his tent to create a dry platform, he curled up and fell fast asleep.

He awoke when the rain stopped. It ended with an abrupt silence, as though someone had turned off a tap. Then the mosquitoes swarmed around him. In a few moments, he was swatting at clouds of them with his hat, regretting that he hadn't brought insect repellent. He ran to the toilet. The ground was a quagmire and in a moment his runners were sodden. A scorpion the size of his fist scuttled across the clearing. In the near darkness of the Relax-Inn, something slid over his foot and he shuddered at its slimy touch.

As he headed back to the tents, he heard a noise. He stopped and held his breath to listen. It could be someone coming to use the toilet, he supposed, but no one appeared on the trail. The compound was deserted. There was only the hissing of puddles as they began to dry, and the slow drip of rain off the trees.

"Hello!" he called.

The noise again. A scraping sound from a food storehouse. Its door swung open. He peered into the shadows, heart beating rapidly. Summoning his courage, he called again, "Hey! Hey you, who are you?"

No answer. He grabbed a broken tree branch off the ground, wielding it in front of him. "Come on out of there!"

A loud screech rent the air as a furry shape dashed out of the hut, swooping for the trees. It sent a shower of raindrops cascading down on him and turned to howl raucous abuse at him from a high branch. In one hand was an apple.

He laughed in relief. A monkey. He'd been afraid of a monkey. He went to shut the storage door, then stopped, his hand on the latch. Wait—the monkey couldn't have opened the door. Someone…He turned around.

Beside the hut, an old man in white baggy shirt and pants and a straw hat was staring at him. Hugh jumped back and raised his stick instinctively.

The man didn't move. Didn't speak.

Hugh lowered the stick. He sensed there was no danger from the old man, so he tried calling to him instead. "Hello. I mean—*buenas tardes*." Hugh approached slowly, not wanting to scare him, then realized he was still holding the stick like a weapon. He dropped it.

The wispy old man seemed to float like a ghost in the heat haze that rose from the steamy ground.

"Senor—" Hugh beckoned, but the old man remained silent.

Yet he heard deep unearthly music from the very air itself and a voice, not the old man's, for his lips never moved, saying, "Welcome. We have been waiting for you, my Lord Jaguar. We have come to take you back with us."

He shook his head to make the voice go away but it persisted.

"The blood of your ancestors soaks the grounds of our fields. The smoke of the usurper hangs in our air. We hear the clarion call of battle but we are nothing without our Lord Jaguar, our hero. Come with us. Your father calls you."

"No, no," he croaked. He forced himself to back away, calling out, "W-who are you? What do you want?"

Silence.

Then a clanging *bong* like the sound of a church bell reverberated through the jungle. The dreamlike atmosphere shattered.

The old man was gone.

There were two large coolers full of beer and soft drinks on the lunchroom table. Hugh dipped his hands into the icy water of one and splashed his face. He shuddered with the sudden cold.

"Welcome back to the real world," Mitch mocked. "Did you have a good sleep?"

"There was an old man. Did you see…?"

She raised a suspicious eyebrow. "Supper's ready." She rang a large bell.

The bell was a magnet drawing the archaeologists back from the digs. Tired and dirty from a day's work under the hot sun, they grabbed their drinks and plopped down at the lunchroom table.

"Say, who are you?" a white-haired man asked. "I'm Dave Kelly."

"Hugh Falkins."

"Roger's son. Oh!"

As all eyes turned on him, Hugh felt as if he were under a microscope.

"Never told us he had a son," snapped a small, thin woman with a hawklike expression. "Not surprising. That man's full of secrets."

"Edith's right," said a young Mexican with a black moustache. "Falkins is keeping secrets from us. I wouldn't be surprised if there's nothing to be found after all. The boy-king's not here and probably never was."

"Garcia, listen." Kelly turned from Hugh and stabbed the table with his finger. "The new glyphs we found clearly show that a temple was built to a new son. Falkins is right."

"Falkins. Falkins. You listen to me; the man's preposterous. He's got us all dreaming of boy-kings. This isn't Egypt, you know."

"But Tutankhamen was real," an attractive woman of about thirty countered. "Howard Carter discovered the Egyptian pharaoh by deciphering ancient ruins, so why not Roger?"

"Joanne, you're bewitched by Falkins," Garcia said, wagging his finger at her. "You won't say anything against him."

The woman blushed and turned her head away.

McVean huffed. "Tactful as usual, Guy. Leave her personal life out of it. You know Roger will find Bird Jaguar's son."

"You mean Shield Jaguar, don't you?" Hugh interjected. "Shield Jaguar was the name of both Bird Jaguar's father and his son."

"Yes, we know that," Kelly said, "but there could be a second son..."

"Wants to keep it for himself," Garcia grumbled.

"That's not fair."

"Oh, stuff it, all of you," Joanne exploded. She ran her fingers through her dishevelled blond hair. "We've had enough for today. At least you can have some consideration for our guest." She turned to Hugh. "Welcome to our camp. I'm Joanne. I have heard of you. Your father speaks very highly of you." She shook his hand gently but with sincerity.

McVean's face reddened. "She's right, of course. Sorry for our bad manners, Hugh. We're a bit testy these days. Should have introduced you properly."

David Kelly was the camp administrator, Guy Garcia an architect specializing in the Mayan region, Edith Richards supervised the collections and Joanne Nielsen, an epigraphist, studied ancient writing. McVean himself, as Mitch had told him, was head of excavations. Oliver Vasquez, a good-looking, middle-aged man with sweeping black hair, was a researcher.

McVean finished his introductions as two more people joined them at the table: Marta Henry, a ceramics specialist, and her husband John, the camp's medical doctor.

"They may look like a pretty ragtag bunch right now," McVean said, "but don't dismiss them lightly. Your father has put together the best brains in the Mayan archaeological business. There's still the survey crew to come in tomorrow—I'm worried that they're late—but that's about everybody. Here we are: Team Yax."

He showed Hugh the words on his soiled T-shirt: "I've been to Yax and Back. Yaxchilán, Chiapas, Mexico."

Hugh gave them a wan smile, uncomfortable with their scrutiny of him, but he knew it wouldn't take long to sort them out, particularly those who seemed belligerent toward his father.

Mitch drew out more cold drinks and banged them on the table. "Supper in a half hour," she announced. She winked at Hugh. The tactic worked, for the drinks cooled off the arguments, and soon afterward the archaeologists left to wash off the sweat and grime of the day. And while they were gone, a group of Mayan men hunched over a small stove at the far end of the clearing. They were local people who came to work as laborers during the day, then return to their villages for the night.

Joanne remained at the table. "Are you on vacation, Hugh?"

"I thought I'd help my dad."

"Joining the slaves then?"

"What do you mean?"

"Archaeology is hard work, not at all glamorous as some people think," she said. "So far we've found dirt, broken rock, more dirt, broken pottery and more dirt again, not to mention snakes, scorpions and beetles. But no temples and definitely no gold."

"I don't think that. I've been on digs with my dad before."

"Funny that Roger didn't mention you were coming. Perhaps he just forgot."

Hugh fidgeted under her stare. "What's an epigraphist? Dr. McVean said you were one."

"Didn't mean to pry," she apologized. "I study Mayan epigraphs, ancient inscriptions on stone."

"Glyphs, you mean?"

"Yes. Hieroglyphs. The Mayans didn't leave us much of a written history but they did record important events on stone. So I study the carvings they made on the buildings and the stelae."

"Stelae?"

"Stone trees. Pillars and blocks of stone. Some are twelve feet high. You'll see them all around the ruins here—sort of an early form of advertising."

"What have you found so far?" Hugh was intrigued.

Joanne's blue eyes misted as if she was looking deep into the past. "Something that doesn't fit. Do you know about the kings of Yaxchilán?"

"Like Shield Jaguar?"

"He was a great old man who lived almost a hundred years. His father, Yat-Balam, started the dynasty of the jaguar kings in AD 320 and his descendants ruled this territory for about five hundred years. Shield Jaguar and his son Bird Jaguar ruled for ninety years between them."

"Then what happened?"

She shrugged. "We don't know. Bird Jaguar's son, Chel-Te, who was also called Shield Jaguar Two after his grandfather, became the last king when he was a boy. Then the dynasty ended."

"So the boy-king the others were arguing about is Shield Jaguar Two?"

Joanne pursed her lips. "No. That's what doesn't fit. Roger thinks that there was another son besides Shield Jaguar Two. He found a buried stela, which suggests that there was a *second* son who led a war against the Totil people. A new temple was being built to glorify him."

Hugh perked up. "Where is it?"

She hesitated. "Er—we can't find it. We should have by now. In fact, the carving on the stones was stopped before completion and then the stones purposely buried."

"Wow!" Hugh licked his lips in anticipation. "Imagine finding his temple. It would be like…"

"Like finding there was another Tutankhamen."

"Yeah. So who was this mysterious third boy-king? Does he have a name?"

"Blood Jaguar."

After the meal and a refreshing shower, Hugh rocked gently in his hammock, fanning himself slowly. Roberto, one of the workers, had set it up for him, slinging the looped ends over hooks screwed into two poles about seven feet apart, letting the remainder hang about three feet off the ground. His first attempts at getting in were embarrassing. Every time he tried to get in lengthways, the hammock slipped out from under him and he fell to the ground. Several other men watched his gymnastics with polite chuckles.

Roberto demonstrated the right way.

Hugh sat sideways on the netting and then twisted himself lengthways, stretching out his long legs. It worked; he was in the hammock, lying back. "Hey, this is great. Thanks."

"Bueno dormido," Roberto said, leaving Hugh to sleep well.

He rocked gently. Heaven, he thought, pure heaven. No more fretting mother, no more scowling Sheldon, no more…

"What the hell are you doing here!"

Hugh jolted out of his reverie with a lurch and fell out of the hammock.

"Answer me!" Hugh's father glared at him, his mouth set in a firm line. He stood with his legs stiffly apart, hands on his hips.

"Dad!" Hugh managed to say lamely. "Uh…hi. Surprise." His heart felt like a stone that dropped straight to his stomach.

At six foot six, Roger Falkins was an imposing, formidable presence anywhere and right now that power hovered directly over Hugh. He scrambled to his feet.

"I'm waiting for a good explanation."

"I—I came for a vacation."

"The school year isn't over yet. You're supposed to be in—" He hesitated. "Is your mother here?"

"No. I came alone."

"With whose permission? Sheldon's?"

"No, Dad. Listen, it was my idea to come. That place was awful. I want to be here, working with you."

"You're going back. The plane will take you back right now. I'm calling—"

The tent door flapped open as Joanne and McVean entered.

"Oh good, Roger." Joanne smiled. "I see you've found him. Oh—" Her face darkened. "What's wrong?"

Hugh's father wagged his finger at Hugh. "I was just telling my surprise visitor he can just pack up and go back with Dario."

"Too late, old man. Plane's gone," McVean said. "Dario won't be back for a few days."

"Then someone can take him back by the road."

"The road's impassable. You know that."

"Mind your own business."

"Roger!" Joanne flared. "That's not fair. Matthew is right. Hugh is here for the night. It's almost suppertime too. We came to get you for supper, Hugh. Let's go eat."

Roger Falkins turned to Hugh. "We'll talk about this later." He pushed his way out of the tent and stamped away.

Team Yax pitched into stuffed chicken *relleno* as if it was their last meal. Hugh's father ate quickly, then left without a word.

Hugh ate listlessly, his eyes lowered. The quiet chitchat about the day's work washed around him: talk of temples, stelae, terracotta pottery and glyphs was scattered with bloodletting, omens and human sacrifice.

A clap of far-off thunder broke the quiet atmosphere. Lightning flashed above the trees and an evening rainstorm began. Unlike the afternoon rain, it was warm and soft. Darkness soon followed as if someone had doused a fire. Mitch lit kerosene lamps, flooding the lunchroom and the surrounding area with a pale glow and a soft hissing sound. Hundreds of insects attracted by the light flitted outside the net walls, but somehow the tiniest mosquitoes found a way through. Hugh's ankles felt as if they were being stabbed by a hundred needles.

"Here, try some of this." John Henry offered him a small bottle.

Hugh poured out a green liquid and rubbed it on his bare ankles and then on his arms for good measure. It gave off a sharp smell. "What is it?"

"Good old-fashioned lime juice mixed with some local leaves. The most ferocious animals in the jungle are not snakes or jaguars, but these nasty little biters." He chuckled. "You'll get used to them. A few days on survey and your blood system will be immune."

"I don't think I'll be staying in Yaxchilán beyond tomorrow," he confided. "My father wants me to go home. And he usually gets his way."

"We'll see about that," Marta replied, pursing her lips. "I'll get Joanne to help. She can usually talk sense into him."

He hoped Joanne could, but he was beginning to think he should be sensible and go home.

Bedtime came early in the jungle. By nine o'clock the archaeologists were asleep and the Mayan workmen, suspicious of the night and its malignant spirits, had already returned to their own village. He tried to sleep but he could not.

A canopy of mosquito netting draped over his hammock made the air hot and stifling. The illuminated dial of his wristwatch showed it was a quarter past nine. Most of his friends would be partying. Right now, they would be stuffing themselves with pizza at the mall and maybe sneaking a few cold beers.

Rain dripped off the leaves. Slithering and chirping noises came from the nearby bush. Branches in the tree above his tent rattled as something scampered through them. He heard a soft grunt.

The old man? He sat upright, waiting for the sound to come again. He felt claustrophobic in the tent, trapped like a caged animal. Pushing aside the mosquito net, he lowered himself out of the hammock and picked up a flashlight Mitch had given him.

"This is crazy," he whispered. "What can I do with a flashlight?" Scarcely daring to breathe, he tiptoed to the tent door, peeking out through the flap. At first, there was nothing unusual, and then he detected a smell like that in the *zocalo* in Villahermosa, the deep pungent smell of a cat. Trembling, he stepped outside.

Above the tent, a jaguar roared into the night, its cry shattering the silence.

Hugh jerked, dropping the flashlight. The light bounced away, slicing through the undergrowth. He stood transfixed with fear, his eyes on the trees above him.

The jaguar growled again, a softer sound this time. Then again, as if trying to speak.

He understood then. The animal was trying to speak to him. His thoughts went out to the cat's as they had done in the marketplace. He knew the jaguar's smell and its roar but he also *felt* its presence. An inexplicable understanding, a closeness, an affinity with the cat. It spoke of power and of danger.

He swayed with dizziness. He was not Hugh Falkins. He was…

The animal grunted once more and, with a spring that sent the tree branches crashing against each other, leaped into the darkness.

Hugh remained alert for a while after that, listening for its return. Its smell lingered in his nostrils and a familiar sense toyed with his subconscious mind. Incomprehensible as it seemed, he had the strangest feeling that he had been warned.

CHAPTER 3

Hugh floated, rocking back and forth with the motion of waves. He lay on the water looking at a sky that could have been the sky at the beginning of time—silent, featureless and endless.

The abrupt *clang* of the breakfast bell woke him.

He was bathed in sweat, his body limp, his head pounding. As he sat upright, the picture of an enormous jaguar with cruel teeth flashed before his eyes, and he was hit with a spear of intense pain.

When the pain subsided he saw that he was rocking in his hammock and morning light played shifting patterns of branches and leaves on the tent canopy.

The bell ran again. Hugh forced himself out of bed.

The sun crested the steep jungle-covered mountains, greeted by parrots and other birds with raucous calls from treetops. Dew was already streaming off the ground though it was only seven A.M.

He considered telling the others about the jaguar but he was sure they'd send him away. Someone who was afraid of shadows would be of no use to them. As for the dream that he was someone else—it was better forgotten.

He was late but the archaeologists were milling about the lunchroom, buzzing with excitement. A jaguar had been heard prowling through the camp during the night.

"I'm afraid." Marta Henry shuddered. "This camp isn't safe any more."

David Kelly put his arm around her shoulders. "Calm down. We're in no danger."

"But what if it attacks us?"

"Wives' tales. You know jaguars aren't aggressive unless provoked."

She grumbled, apparently not convinced, nor did the others look any more comfortable.

A wild screech ripped through air. Edith Richards screamed and her coffee cup fell to the ground with a crash.

Guy Garcia, at the end of the table, laughed. He held a strange looking object—a gourd cut open at one end with a tightly stretched leather cover

over the other. Down through the middle of the gourd, hanging from the leather lid, was a piece of rigid waxed cord that he plucked through the open end. It emitted a ferocious, high-pitched squeal.

"Good God—what on earth is that?" Matthew McVean gasped.

"It's a jaguar caller." He stroked it again, bringing forth a low vibrating sound, almost a growl.

Hugh felt a tremor of recognition run through him.

"You scared us to half to death with that thing. Put it away!" Joanne demanded.

Garcia continued to strum the object. "Amusing, isn't it? It's the mating call of the male jaguar, Joanne. Perhaps it is calling *you-u-u-u*," he joked. "Don't you find it appealing?"

"The only sound you could make that would appeal to me is the sound of your hasty retreat. I said—put it away."

"As you wish, *Doctor*," he retorted. He stood up abruptly and strode out of the compound.

McVean mocked Garcia's angry expression. "Well done, Joanne. I don't care for that man. We have enough trouble with one animal."

Joanne said, "I don't understand why a jaguar would come through an area with so many humans in it. They usually stay away."

Kelly shrugged. "I don't know either. But just to be safe, I want everyone to take a gun. I don't expect to have any prob—"

"Senors! Senors!"

Roberto, the Mayan workman, ran toward the lunchroom, his eyes wide with terror, as he jabbered something in Spanish so fast Hugh couldn't make sense of it.

Hugh's father, attracted by the commotion, shouldered his way through the group. "What goes on here?"

Roberto let loose another tumble of Spanish, his chest heaving, his hands waving wildly.

"Roberto, *más despacioso, por favor.* Slower, please. What's the matter?" He steered the workman to a seat.

Roberto, trembling, wringing his hat nervously, told his story in halting English. A jaguar had attacked one of the men coming to work.

"Attacked? Is he hurt?"

"Yes. You must hurry."

John Henry immediately went for his medical bag.

"This is bad, Senor Falkins," Roberto said. "The jaguar does not attack a man. He must be a *brujo*."

"Nonsense. There are no sorcerers here, Roberto."

"We want to leave, Senor. Too many bad things happen here."

"You must stay."

"No." Roberto blanched. "The old women in the village are afraid. It is *Uayeb*—the evil days. We want to go."

Hugh's father stiffened. "Five more days, Roberto. That's all we have left to work here and that will be the end of your contract. If you want to be paid, you'll stay."

"But, Senor..."

"No more! We've had enough slowdowns as it is, and I won't have a bunch of faint-hearted cowards running out on me because some old village witch-women say so. Doctor Henry will see to the hurt man and you have your own work to do. I won't hear any more about sorcerers or evil days. And I won't have any more interference. *Vamos!* Let's go!"

The others took the hint to go too; only McVean, Mitch and Hugh remained.

"What's this business about *Uayeb?*" Hugh asked Matthew McVean.

"The five unlucky days. Do you know anything about the Mayan calendar?"

"No."

Mitch guffawed. "Get ready for a history lesson."

McVean waved her comment aside good-naturedly, sipping his coffee before launching into his explanation. "The ancient Maya were a very remarkable people, you know. They had incredible skills in mathematics, astronomy and calendaring, even when Europe was in the Dark Ages. In fact, they had three calendars."

Hugh listened closely.

"Imagine having a year of eighteen months instead of twelve, and twenty days to a month. That's the *Haab,* totalling three hundred and sixty days. The remaining five days are the *Uayeb*."

His eyes flickered with mischief and his voice deepened. He leaned toward Hugh. "These five days were so dangerous and unlucky that the Maya fasted and obeyed sacred rules to prevent any disaster from occurring."

Mitch emitted a low howl. "Beware! Beware!"

But Hugh was not amused. He felt a dark shadow pass over him. "That workman was afraid. I mean, really afraid."

"They're superstitious," McVean replied. "Every day was governed by a special god who made that day good luck or bad luck. So they created the *Tzolkin* calendar of two hundred and sixty days to help them predict a good luck or bad luck day and make the right prayers to placate the god."

"Then you wouldn't want to be born on a bad day."

"For sure. You'd have bad luck for your whole life. So you'd want to pick a good day, say, for the birth of a child or the planting of crops. Even to decide when it would be safe to go to war. Good or bad events would occur again and again."

Hugh wondered if today was good luck for him.

McVean finished his coffee. "Old superstition dies hard out here. This is not the big city. We could lose those workmen if they believe the bad days are coming, so that's why your father was right to insist we finish our work."

"Though," he continued thoughtfully, "I'm not always so sure that our bad luck isn't caused by the gods."

"You said there were three calendars."

"Yes, meshing the two calendars together made another way of telling time, the Calendar Round, which lasted fifty-two years. At the end of each fifty-two-year cycle, the *Tun*, the Mayans predict a time of monumental upheaval and catastrophe—"

"Hi, everyone!"

A man and woman strode into the compound followed by a troop of workers carrying tents and excavation equipment.

"Ah, the expeditionary force into the wilds of the Chiapas jungle returns," McVean declared. "How went the battle?"

"I've discovered three new species of mosquito and two unknown varieties of stinging nettles," the woman groaned, plopping herself down on the lunchroom bench. About twenty-five, she was slim, with a punk haircut and an earring in her nose. She wore mottled green army fatigues.

Her companion, a Mexican a few years older than her, was dressed as if he was posing for *National Geographic* in safari bush jacket and pith helmet. When he removed the helmet, he revealed a neatly combed wave of black hair. He sprawled in the chair, long legs sticking out under the table.

McVean introduced Linda Chandler and Jose Morales.

Jose smiled expansively at Mitch. *"Dos Equis,* two beers." He held up two fingers. "To hail the conquering explorers."

"Sure. Coming right up. We wondered why you guys were late. What happened?"

"We got held up. Literally," Linda grumbled. "The Mexican army wouldn't let us move camp for two days."

"Army?"

"Looking for rebels." She turned to Hugh. "The river is the border between Mexico and Guatemala, you know. They've been fighting for control of this land since 1980."

"Warned us not to leave until they scouted the whole area," Jose scoffed. "They're afraid of their own shadows."

Armies? Guerrillas? A war? Hugh felt a tremor of uneasiness.

"I hope they don't come this far," McVean said. "Things are bad enough here as it is. By the way, where's Schele?"

"Who knows? Who cares? He high-tailed it somewhere just before we got back. Said he'd be along later."

"Hartmann Schele," Mitch explained for Hugh's benefit. "Director of surveys, their boss. A real pain in the behind."

"Well put, my pretty," Jose agreed. "If I don't see him for another week, that won't be long enough. I need a long rest."

He and Linda finished their drinks and immediately headed off to wash and sleep.

As Hugh watched them go, he realized they had not expressed surprise or concern that he was Roger Falkins' son. He said so to Mitch.

She shrugged. "No reason they should. So you're here for a visit, nothing unusual about that, is there? You aren't the center of our universe."

He wasn't sure if Mitch was rebuking him but it occurred to him that maybe she was right. There was nothing unusual. He shouldn't be so uptight.

The thought gladdened him.

Great temples of white stone rose from a wide plaza fronting the river, through steep terraced hills, and then further inland into thicker jungle. To the east, the gleaming Usumascinta River curved around the ruins in an oxbow formation, as if holding them in its arms.

Hugh decided to explore. He chose a trail that took him down toward the river and the ruins of Yaxchilán, ancient city of the Maya.

He wandered down to the plaza, between empty columns that once supported roofs, over ceremonial platforms, and into small buildings where mysterious interiors lay hidden in darkness. Everywhere, jungle encroached. It crept around, under and over platforms, walls, doorways and posts like a subtle green army. He found it exciting, haunting.

There were no high-pointed Egyptian pyramids. These were rectangular buildings with loaf-shaped roofs, made of white limestone glinting in the sun. Scattered throughout the plaza were carvings and glyphs—on stone altars, poles and panels. He was astounded by the sculptures of Mayan men in plumed headdresses and short kilts. Their faces were carved with receding foreheads and long noses and their eyes were narrow, hostile slits. Most held swords, clubs or spears in their hands.

"It isn't possible," he said, "but I feel as if I've been here before. If stones could speak..."

His throat went dry, his eyes misted. He gripped the edge of an altar, trying to hold back the noises which began in his head—a pounding drum, clashing of cymbals, a long, drawn out, melancholy note like a fog horn. And voices, voices that reached out to him with their eerie, ghostly whisper and pulled memories from deep within his mind.

He felt faint.

Human figures, like the ones he saw on the Cessna, took shape before his eyes, wavering, struggling to become real. When the thin mist parted, crowds of people thronged the plaza shore, waiting for a boat to come upriver. They wore robes and plumed headdresses of iridescent feathers, a flock of colorful birds. Behind them, gleaming white citadels ascended forested hills in broad, massive terraces to the tallest bluffs; not ruins at all. They could have been built yesterday and the jungle cleared around them.

Trumpets rang from the temple walls, echoing up the river canyon.

"He comes. He comes," the crowd shouted. "*Halach unic! Halach unic!*"

A massive canoe rounded the curve of the river, resplendent in a canopy of gold. Rows of men raised and dipped their paddles in unison. Sitting on a raised seat was the king.

The king. Hugh yearned to see his face. He leaned forward, pressed by the crush of bodies. He flushed with warmth, his head reeling, eyes glazed. Then he collapsed.

"Hey! Hey, wake up!"

A giant mosquito stung his face. He woke with a jolt, his head spinning. Sharp sunlight stabbed his eyes. When it stopped, Mitch was helping him to his feet. He nearly fell again but she held him up and pressed a water bottle to his lips.

He drank deeply. The cold water cleared his head.

"Hey! You okay?"

"Yeah. I must have fainted."

"Man, you were delirious. Where's your hat?"

It lay on the ground beside him. He shoved it on quickly, receiving another stab of pain for the effort.

"You gotta watch it out here," she said. "This sun's a real killer. Only a real *gringo* would be out here at midday. What were you doing, anyway? You were shouting. You're sure you're okay?"

He waved aside her question and dragged himself into the shade of a wall, waiting for the dizzy feeling to pass. It occurred to him that he'd been doing a lot of fainting lately and it wasn't all due to the heat. Something was definitely wrong but he wasn't going to admit it to Mitch.

"I'm better now. Thanks."

She let him drink all the water, watching him with a puzzled look on her face. "Strange, you know."

"What is?"

"You suddenly showing up and your dad not knowing. Why *are* you here?"

"A visit."

"Sure. And you're Sam Sheldon's stepson. And he's coming in a few days. You..."

"You think I'm his spy. Is that it? Well, I'm not. I don't even like the man."

"Okay, okay. Don't get huffy. It's just coincidental, that's all."

He turned away from her, staring out into the compound. The hot sun beat down on the plaza, glaring off white limestone.

"Hey, look," she said finally, "I'm sorry, okay? I didn't mean to get personal. It's just that I wouldn't put it past Sheldon to spy on us. And...and you sound like your dad."

He waited for her to go on.

She deliberately turned her head away. "He hears things. Voices. Like he's psychic or something. He even sees things."

He felt a cold shadow pass over him. "What things? How do you know?"

She looked back reluctantly. "Well, he's pretty careful not to let the others see him, them being scientists and all, but I saw him—when he couldn't see me—and he talks to himself."

"Everyone does," he scoffed.

"Not ancient Mayan—I know a few words. It's like he's holding a conversation with someone but no one else is there."

Hugh fanned himself with his hat, thinking rapidly. If his father heard voices, then he could have also. The thought shocked him, disturbed him.

"Who do you think he was he talking to?"

"Ghosts."

He pretended scorn. "Oh, c'mon now."

"Of course you're skeptical. But it's—it's too real. I almost believe they're there. I think they show him things."

"Like buried treasure."

"Like Lady's grave," she said pointedly. "We must have walked over it a hundred times and then he found it just as easy as a diviner finds water."

"He's just good at that sort of stuff. Has been all his life. I once hid some magazines—well, you know the kind—but he found them right away. I think I still have the scars here." He rubbed his bottom in demonstration.

Mitch smiled. "You like him. But do you believe me?"

Hugh nodded. He cleared his throat. "So, now it's my turn to grill you—how come you're here with *your* father? That's pretty odd too."

She laughed. "I'm daddy's boy: 'Give it to Mitch to do. My right hand man. Mitch can fix it. Mitch can cook it...' Speaking of which, I've got to get lunch ready."

He was determined not to let her off the hook that easily.

"Where's your mother?"

"Dead. Oh, don't look surprised. She died when I was a baby, so it's not like I've ever had a mother."

"It's been tough, I suppose."

"It's been—okay."

They stood up together, facing each other in silence, assessing each other, but the tension was gone.

Abruptly, Mitch yanked her hat down on her head. "Gotta go make lunch. See you later."

Hugh watched her go up the trail to the tent site, his mind turning over the things she said about his father. But he couldn't make sense of them. Maybe she had been trying to start a fight. Maybe she was lonely.

Like him.

Hugh saw his father walking across the plaza. He waited nervously.

But his father calmly pulled out his favorite pipe from his shirt pocket and began to stuff it with tobacco, taking his time. He waited until he had produced a satisfactory plume of smoke before speaking.

"Thought I might find you here."

"I'm only looking around. Nothing else to do." Hugh tried to keep his voice casual and relaxed.

"They're dangerous, these old places. Lots of crumbling masonry. Spiders. Snakes too. But interesting, don't you think?" He puffed contentedly on the pipe, surveying the plaza and the surrounding terraces as if he owned the place. "Yaxchilán. Or in ancient Mayan, Malenche, the place of the green stones. Actually, the stones in the river bed are just covered with green algae."

Hugh smiled.

"Look, I'm sorry I was rough on you last night. You gave me quite a shock, showing up here."

"Sorry, I thought you'd be pleased to see me."

"I am. I am. But—well, you don't know how rough it's been here. Difficult. And we're on a tight schedule. So you see…Oh, c'mon, I'll show you around."

They moved out of the shade.

"This is the main ceremonial plaza. You could fit three football fields on it though you wouldn't know they were here because the jungle grows over it so fast. In Malenche's heyday, this would have been completely cleared."

"When was that?"

"Eighth century. The religious temples and altars would be doing a brisk daily business. And up there about three hundred feet,"—the pipe had gone out but he used it to point to the slope behind the plaza—"are more ceremonial buildings. You could have climbed those stairs to the top."

"But why build way up there anyway?"

"Temples and residences for the elite—the *h'menob* and the *ahauob*. It's much cooler up there and it dries out faster in the rain. Fewer mosquitoes too. That's also why we made camp higher up. All the lower classes lived in wooden huts along the bench of the river."

Hugh was thinking about Sam Sheldon, whose mansion overlooked Tampa Bay. Sheldon had probably talked to his father by now, even made plans to have Hugh sent back. His mother would be missing him.

He pushed the thoughts to the back of his mind as they continued to walk along the plaza. He was happy to let his father do the talking.

"Here's where all the action was. Everything was carried by boat, so the riverfront was a harbor, trade center, meeting place and bus station all in one. Many of these smaller buildings, like the one you were standing in, were stores."

They stopped at one carved with inscriptions on the outside walls, lintels, stairways and porticoes. A doorway led into a dark corridor.

His father cleared a spider's web with a tree branch before entering. From his pocket he produced a flashlight, and shone its light on the roof and walls of the empty chamber.

"The inner rooms are dark and cool because there are no windows. Only a small air vent kept them cool and dry." His voice echoed off the high ceiling. "Watch out for the bat dung."

Hugh ran his hand over the carvings. One depicted a kneeling man receiving a string of beads from a dignitary in ceremonial headdress. Even though it was stone, the carving seemed alive under his fingers. He wouldn't have been surprised to see the kneeling man rise up and bow.

"Shield Jaguar, the old king himself," his father said as if he knew the stone figure personally. "Ruled here for ninety years before passing his kingdom to his son. He was revered as a god and loved as a king, but his enemies would have respected his power too. A dangerous man."

Hugh heard the breath of excitement in his father's voice and discovered that he, too, was tingling with interest.

Outside, brilliant sunlight momentarily blinded them. They walked toward two large rectangles bordered by high sloping walls. Wind hummed through the empty space like a crowd hushed with anticipation. Hugh felt afraid even with his father present.

"Do you know what these are?"

"Basketball courts?" he ventured.

"Not basketball. The Mayans' game was called *pok-a-tok;* the ball players could use only their fists, elbows and hips to try and drive a hard rubber ball through those two end zones."

"I've seen pictures. They tried to put the ball through a ring in the wall, right?"

"You're thinking of the Aztec version of the game. Think of a combination of football and basketball with no rules."

"Ouch!"

His father grinned mischievously. "Not as dangerous as losing the game. The winner was elevated to the status of a god but the loser lost the game and all his equipment to the other side. Then he was sacrificed."

Hugh's stomach did a queasy flip. He could imagine the crowds shouting for blood, while the king, from his throne, watched the deadly struggles of his warriors below. "This is an amazing place," he said at last, though *amazing* wasn't what he was thinking. He was thinking—dangerous, fatal.

His father took a great deal of time to relight his pipe, sending blue smoke into the air. "Unfortunately, it's the last time you'll see it this way before they build a good road from Villahermosa. Then it'll just be another damn tourist attraction."

He understood his father's resentment but he said, "If you find Blood Jaguar, the tourists will come in droves."

"The boy-king. Yes, they'll come then." His father sniffed the air as if that ancient person might suddenly materialize. "He's here. I can feel him as if he's standing beside me."

"You hear him, too."

His father raised an eyebrow. "I'm a scientist, not a ghost hunter."

"But you do?"

"I don't hear or see things and I don't make them up, either. But there's more to this world than meets the eye or the imagination. I'll find him." He clenched the pipe between his teeth hard. "I have to."

"Mitch said—"

"I've been patient with you. You owe me an explanation about how you came to be here."

Hugh realized his father was right. He took a deep breath. "I left on my own. I paid my own airfare."

"Without telling anyone or asking permission? Least of all, Sam's?"

Hugh couldn't find the right words to say.

"Sam Sheldon is your guardian. However much you may dislike him, you owe him your duty. And your mother."

Hugh only stared.

"Now see here," he pointed the pipestem, "Sam is also our benefactor. Without his money, the project fails. And if he finds you here, it will jeopardize everything."

"I'll help you."

"You're not capable."

"I have experience. You taught me yourself."

"But not Mayan—" He hesitated. His eyes softened and he looked off into the far hills. When he spoke, his voice was weary. "Look, I know it must be tough on you but your mother and I had this out a long time ago. Decisions were made."

"It's fine for her. She's happy."

"I'm glad. But you've got to go back. Your mother would never forgive me if something happened to you. And I'd blame myself. No, you're going to have to go."

CHAPTER 4

"We're right in the middle of a war and we'd better get out now." Hartmann Schele, the director of surveys, slammed his fist on the lunchroom table, making the dust rise. "We could be killed in the crossfire."

Hugh went cold. Schele's voice was thick with anger, his face, in the wan light of the kerosene lamps, hard and cruel.

The faces of the archaeologists were drawn and worried. David Kelly brushed a hand through his white hair in frustration. "Hartmann," he said, "I've no doubt what you say is true. But the Mexican army is probably just on a routine patrol. Rebels are common in the area, and besides, we've never been bothered before."

"I tell you their soldiers were equipped for all out war. That was no ordinary troop movement my crew saw this afternoon. Something big is going to happen."

Joanne saw the look on Hugh's face. She leaned over and whispered to him, "Apparently Guatemalan rebels have crossed the river to the Mexican side."

Hugh said, "Are we in danger?"

"Schele wants us to pack up and go home."

Kelly was livid. "We've survived worse than this. There's too much at stake here to run off like scared rabbits. We stay unless Roger says otherwise."

"Ha. That fool. He'll never leave until he's found his precious boy-king. He doesn't care if the rest of us are in danger. He should be here now to get us out of this mess."

It was clear to Hugh that Schele was taking advantage of his father's absence to malign him, accusing him of deserting his team. Hugh groaned inwardly, remembering his father's words about Blood Jaguar only that afternoon. *I'll find him. I have to.*

Marta Henry said, "Maybe Hartmann is right. But we're so close."

"I won't give up now," Joanne said flatly.

"Four more days," Kelly pleaded. "Then we have to pack up anyway."

The others nodded in agreement.

Schele grumbled but he knew he'd lost the argument. He left without saying more.

Hugh watched him go. The man made him feel uneasy, as if...

"Are you all right?" Joanne put her hand on his. Her eyes were soft and concerned. "It will all be over in a few days. So don't worry."

He slumped in his chair. It was all right for her to talk about leaving soon. But he was going to be given the heave-ho before the project even ended, before he really had a chance to convince his father not to send him back.

The kerosene lamp sputtered. Mitch pumped the handle and it flared into new life, casting back the shadows. The archaeologists were arguing with each other.

"...there's always been war here. King Bird Jaguar defeated the Totil army to establish his son on the throne."

"...of course, but he was strong enough to withhold any major attack."

"...he was weakened by the nobles who wanted his power. There were those who wanted to see his lineage come to an end."

"...too many taxes. The people revolted."

Joanne chuckled. "Confusing, isn't it? No one really knows why Bird Jaguar's realm suddenly collapsed, Hugh. They'll certainly never figure it out this evening. Besides, we like arguing; it's our form of television out here in the jungle."

Hugh was too tired to try to make sense of the arguments.

He went back to his tent and swung gently in his hammock for his last night in the jungle. The saw of the cicadas and the buzz of the mosquitoes on the other side of his screen reminded him that the jungle had existed, would exist, longer than man. The kings were dead. All that was left were ruins and ghosts. The Maya had believed the world was created and destroyed four times before humans made an appearance. If the world was destroyed again, he would not be surprised.

Hugh heard a noise. He was instantly alert, anticipating the growl of the jaguar again. The stillness was ominous—no ruffle of feathers from the sleeping birds overhead, no rustle of leaves from a breeze. The rain had not yet come but he could smell it in the air.

He stepped out of the tent. A pale moon fought with ragged clouds in the night sky, giving enough light to see the outlines of objects. He thought he saw a shadow moving on the trail. The old man then? This time he'd catch him in the act of stealing and then, because he felt sorry for him, he'd give him something to eat from the lunchroom. Surely there was no need for him to have to act like a thief.

He returned for his shoes and then padded off in pursuit. When he passed the other tents, rumbles and wheezes told him the archaeologists were fast asleep and he paused beside his father's tent but heard no sound coming from it.

He went up the trail toward the higher placed ruins. He stopped once or twice to listen and assure himself that his "shadow" was still ahead but the unknown figure could be distinctly heard, apparently unconcerned about making noise once it was beyond hearing range of the camp. When the trail broke out into the open, he saw it move quickly toward the door of a small temple.

In the moonlight, the ruins gave off an eerie whiteness like old bones. Hugh crept around the open area, keeping to the dark, and approached the building from the side. His heart began to beat rapidly and, in spite of the cool evening, he was sweating. Creeping as close to the front as possible, he hid in the thick jungle foliage.

A lamp sputtered to life. It spread a pool of light in front of the door and he saw a hand and leg moving. And then another. A second person had joined the lantern-bearer. Insects, attracted by the light, also began to move in.

Mosquitoes lanced Hugh's ankles but his fear of discovery held back his desire to swat at them. He couldn't move now. A drop of sweat trickled down his forehead and dripped into his eyes. Lightning flashed silently and, a few seconds later, thunder rumbled on the distant horizon.

In low but distinct voices, the figures began speaking in Spanish. As one of them stepped further into the lantern-light, he caught a momentary glint of metal. A woman. The light flashed off her earrings.

A rendezvous then? He wondered if he was watching a local girl who had slipped out to meet her lover under cover of darkness. Or perhaps it was an archaeologist, Joanne or Linda. Well, yes—Mitch, too.

The unknown couple waited. He breathed as calmly as he could. Thunder rolled again and clouds began to blank out the moon that had been clear a moment ago.

A third figure appeared out of the darkness, announcing itself with a low cough. Their conversation, directed away from him, came in snatches, this time in Spanish, some English. He couldn't recognize the muffled voices or see the face of the new arrival.

"...taking them out...I'm sure of it...five days...deadline..."

Hugh strained to hear. He stepped forward for a better look. In doing so, he nudged loose a stone that rattled loudly.

He quickly flattened himself against the wall, holding his breath, waiting to be discovered. Lightning flashed far away but the figures had gone.

In their place came the ghost.

Low voices, accompanied by the steady beat of drum and jangle of beads, came from the temple. They escalated in volume until they became the throbbing, pounding rhythm of a dirge. Hugh stood transfixed as the sound ran over his body like electricity.

White smoke issued from the ground and pale light rose with it, lighting the area in an eerie, spectral aura. A tall figure appeared in the mist, bodiless at first, then becoming distinct as it came nearer—a Mayan warrior, floating through the white light, his head covered by a huge helmet made in the snarling profile of a jaguar, his body encased in padded armor. One hand held a rectangular shield, the other a huge club.

Hugh ran. Oblivious to the branches that slashed at his bare arms and face, he barrelled through the underbrush, slipping in the mud. His blood screamed in his ears. He could almost hear the swish of the massive club through the air.

He dove into the trees off the trail and seconds later heard the warrior charge past him.

He gasped for air. His lungs ached but he couldn't stop now. His only chance was to head back the opposite way, and he ran again. Straight into someone who loomed out of the darkness.

They yelled in frightened unison. A fist came out of the darkness, smacking him in the jaw. He went down like a felled log.

He expected the thump of the club but none came. As quickly as he had encountered the shadowy figure, it was gone. But he wasn't going to wait around. Panting heavily, he ran back for the camp. When he tripped over something in the darkness, a voice shouted at him in a muffled voice to watch where he was going.

Thank goodness, he sighed. He was back. He'd only tripped on a guy rope supporting one of the tents. But no one came out to investigate. As quietly as possible, he slipped into his own tent. Some time later, he dared to poke his head out of the tent. Exhausted, he peeled off his wet clothes and towelled down.

The sweat and the chill of fear would not leave him, though. Ghosts. Ridiculous, he told himself; there are no ghosts. He had seen real people and a real person had hit him. His jaw still hurt. There had to be a more rational explanation for what he had seen.

He went to bed immediately. But he was afraid.

"Rise and shine. It's six-thirty," someone yelled in Hugh's ear, the sound insistent and cheerful.

He threw off the blanket and rose stiffly, stumbling to the tent door, his head thick with the sludge of sleep. He blinked in the bright morning sunlight.

Linda Chandler was standing there, her arms crossed and a humorous expression on her mouth. "C'mon there, sleepyhead," she chirped, "time to get going."

"Going?" his voice was thick and groggy. "Where?"

"Your old man's given us permission to take you on survey. A trek into the deepest, darkest, most dangerous jungles of Mexico in search of lost cities of gold. *Andale.* Move it. Breakfast's almost ready."

He surged with excitement. He could stay! He hurried into some fresh clothes and washed up quickly. His jaw hurt a bit but otherwise seemed not to have suffered any serious damage. He hoped it wasn't bruised. In the clear light of day his nocturnal adventure suddenly seemed childish. He considered telling his father but as he hurried to the lunchroom, he squashed that idea. If his father had given him a chance to stay, he didn't want to ruin it by making up a preposterous sounding story of a secret rendezvous at night.

Mitch was in a growly mood. Her hair was tousled and her eyes baggy. She looked as though she hadn't slept.

"Where are the others?" he asked, digging into warm bacon and eggs.

"Already gone," she mumbled. "It's seven o'clock. We get up at six around here. This isn't a hotel, you know."

He gulped down his breakfast, avoiding her look, then went over to Linda and Jose who were packing equipment.

"So where are we going?" he asked, barely concealing his anticipation.

Jose said, "Only a few miles north of here where there's an old wellsite. The people of the village have been using it for hundreds of years and it could be evidence of former occupation. We can't leave any stone unturned, so to speak." He hefted a huge pack onto his back as if he was going on a Sunday outing.

"Here's yours." Linda kicked over a smaller pack. "Just lunch, some water and a few tools." She checked her watch. "Joanne's going to join us later, and who knows, maybe even Schele."

Hugh was given a pair of rubber boots, a work shirt, work gloves, a pair of baggy khakis and a hammock. He asked about the boots.

"For the rain, of course," Linda explained, "but there are all kinds of creepy-crawlies out there in the bush including venomous snakes and scorpions. That's why you've got the gloves, too. We'll be prodding around a lot of loose rock lying on the jungle floor."

"And the hammock?"

"When it's time for siesta, you don't want to be on the ground." She zigzagged her hand to indicate snake. Lifting her own pack as easily as Jose had his, she looked ready for a hardy expedition.

Before they left, Jose strapped a businesslike pistol around his waist.

Hugh stared at it.

"It's a jungle out there." Jose smiled at his own joke but his expression was serious. "There's no one you can run to for help. Our short wave radios have limited range. So if there's a problem, you've got to take care of it yourself."

Great, Hugh was thinking. Scorpions, snakes, guerrillas. What other dangers did the jungle hide?

Mitch saw them off. "See you at supper." She snickered at Hugh. "Watch out for surprises."

For the next hour, he immersed himself in the wonders of the lowland jungle. They walked a narrow trail that rose slowly but steadily into the mountains. The *monte*, thickets of fern, bamboo and dead tree trunks draped with looping vines, made an impenetrable wall around them. Where the trail had already lost the steamy haze of the morning dew, the shaggy, shaded undergrowth sparkled with water droplets and a profusion of colors—red and yellow fruit, pink and purple orchids, and white bromeliads. Green ferns, tropical fungi and vines as thick as his arm competed for space, each searching for the elusive sun. The rank smell of rotting vegetation was powerful.

Jose and Linda were encyclopedias of information—they showed him the 400-foot *guanacaste* tree whose trunk was three times the width of his outstretched arms, musky pods underneath the wide canopy of the *bokut* giving it the name "stinking toe," black oozing sap from the poisonwood tree, and the tall *cohune* palm with a thick trunk and elegant plumed fronds.

Animals were more difficult to see. He could hear the ear-shattering calls of the howler monkey but saw only black blurry shapes in the forest canopy. Parrots and birds flashed across his vision and exotic butterflies flitted across the trail to disappear in the dark jungle. Lizards basked on tree trunks exposed to the sun. In a single movement, they vanished as if they never existed. Only once did he see a mammal, a portly tapir, but the piglike animal simply ignored them and crashed its way into the undergrowth before it, too, was gone.

Jose suddenly stopped, pointing at the ground. "You won't see that on the streets of New York City," he said.

Hugh craned forward to see. A column of small leaves no wider than his thumb was marching across the trail. The line was endless.

"What are they?" he asked and bent down for a closer inspection.

"Leaf-cutter ants. Here, watch." Jose placed a branch across the trail.

He could see now that each leaf was being carried by a small ant in a line going one way while another parallel line returned to the source of the leaves. When they reached the branch, they milled around in confusion for a few moments but quickly regained rank and file and continued their parallel ways *over* the branch.

"Amazing!"

"They'll do that all day and night," Linda said. "They eat hundreds of pounds in a day just to feed themselves."

"Yeech."

"Not to the ants. It's actually the fungus that grows on the leaves that they crave. It's just like caviar to them."

"This place is great."

"Just wait 'til you see the quetzal," Jose said. "Its feathers are like rainbows. The ancient Mayan nobles made headdresses and cloaks out of them."

They continued on their way and soon the *monte* flattened out into wide areas where thinner trees and shorter grasses grew. Unprotected by the thicker growth through which he had come, Hugh found the sun hot and bright. He was tired and thirsty too. Linda and Jose were careful to arrange for water breaks along the way.

Finally, they reached an area of open land populated with pockets of jungle and thin scrub. The land was bumpy with overgrown tussocks and mounds of grass. At one end, protected under the shade, was a large well made from loose stones.

"What are we looking for?"

"Temples."

"Up here?"

Jose laughed. "Every mound is a temple, every rock is a temple until we prove otherwise. There could have been temples up here. Over the years the stones would have been taken away to make other buildings and fences. And erosion would have done its part, too. But what we really want is evidence of a village."

Using a large tree as a benchmark, they strung off a huge area into a grid and, in parallel rows, they began to search the ground for carved stones or clearly defined building blocks. If they found artifacts from an ancient village, they would measure the position on the grid and note it on a graph in Linda's field notebook.

Hugh was using his spade to clear debris away from a hole in the ground when something green flashed out at him.

He screamed, jumping back instinctively. The green arrow glanced off the steel of his spade with a resounding *thud.* He barely took it in before the slithering shape disappeared in the tall grass. A hot flush of adrenaline shot through his body.

"S-snake," he croaked.

Jose watched the snake speed away, his hand poised on the pistol. "Green adder. Very poisonous. You must be careful," he warned.

Hugh gulped. But he watched with more attention thereafter.

Even so, the work was hot, sticky and repetitive—hours of climbing over rocks and tussocks, ducking branches, trudging back and forth to measure—all under the relentless sun. Flies hovered around his eyes while mosquitoes and other insects danced and buzzed around his body with irritating persistence. Sweat trickled down his forehead and into his eyes. He was ready to give up.

"Hey! Look!" Linda shouted, pointing at something under a large decayed tree.

As he and Jose rushed to see, Hugh became excited at the thought of what she'd found, visions of another skeleton like Lady dancing in his head.

Linda pointed to a wide, circular depression, partially hidden by a fallen tree. She took out a trowel and began to carefully dig around the roots to get a closer look. As she scraped with her trowel, they heard a hollow sound. "There's something under here!" she exclaimed.

Hugh held his breath as Linda cleared away the dirt, revealing colorful fragments of clay.

"Just a bunch of broken pots," he said.

"Potsherds." Jose's voice rose in anticipation. "Don't be disappointed. This is a good sign."

"More than that," Linda breathed excitedly. "See? On the side—those painted designs? Post-classic Yuum Kaax, I'm sure."

Jose explained. "Yuum Kaax, the God of Maize or Corn. Those designs on the rim of the bowl are very similar to those we found on the plaza below and very definitely the post-classic time period, about 700 to 800 AD."

"Which means the same people as those in the site below," Linda added.

Hugh remembered now what his father had told him. Potsherds were like fragments of Coca-Cola bottles on the moon—evidence of the existence of real people. His body trembled with the pleasure of the hunt.

He and Jose carefully lifted the decayed tree and moved it aside to reveal a huge depression. They stood back as ants, chiggers, beetles and other insects scrambled for cover. There were no snakes.

But there were more potsherds. Hundreds of them.

"Could be a *midden*," Linda said. "A sort of garbage dump. What they threw out tells us a great deal about them—what they ate, what they wore..."

"And Bird Jaguar?" Hugh prompted.

Jose chuckled. "Who knows? Maybe his favorite smoking pipe."

They cleared a wide area (enough to prove that the depression was indeed a *midden*), before they broke for lunch, resting against the cool stones of a large well shaded by a massive ceiba tree. The well was called Chac Puuc, after Chac, the Rain God. Puuc was a spirit of underground streams and wells. Hugh was impressed, for the well was easily six to eight feet in diameter and about thirty feet deep. The surface was six feet below the rim of the well where Hugh could hear the gurgling of water from an underground system.

"Maybe now we can convince Sheldon to come back next year," Linda said firmly.

Jose was doubtful. "Garbage pits and old pots don't bring in the big bucks. We'll have to find something really spectacular, something glamorous, to convince him that our work is worthwhile."

The sun was high overhead. Hugh was tired, his body unused to the strains of survey work. Shutting his eyes, he forgot about stringing his hammock as he slipped into a light sleep. Against his back the coolness of the stones was a physical hand, rubbing his spine, soothing his fears. Light played against his face with cooling, soothing fingers. A soft melody was coming *through* the stone walls of the well—the slow, persistent sound of a flute, and with it a voice singing in a sweet falsetto scarcely higher than the expelling of a breath.

The voice was female, a young woman. She was singing to him, calling him by a different name. He couldn't hear it but he knew it was his. He strained to hear. Her voice was beautiful, comforting, rising like a bird on the winds of the flute. The jungle held its breath to hear, too. Then her tone changed. It warbled; it trembled like a reed in the wind. It shrilled in desperation and pain.

It was drowned out by the voices of men. They came from deep inside him, burbling out of his throat. *"Akab. Akab d'zib."* He heard them like a litany and he repeated them. *"Itzamna. Ix Chel. Kinich Ahau."* Like a horrible curse, *"Xibalba. Xibalba. Xibalba."*

Growing louder. The drumbeats stronger. Shadows, like giant wings, beat against him.

His voice rose to a screaming, defiant pitch. His body twisted and fought against them.

He yelled, "Hail to One Death. Hail to Seven Death. Hail Skull. Bloody Claws. I have come to defeat you."

The sky splintered with light. A grotesque, scarred face with bulging eyes and a hooked nose stared into his and a deep, cold voice rumbled. "Who comes to *Xibalba*? Who defies *Ah Puch*, the God of Death?"

CHAPTER 5

A livid, angry face hovered above his, its lips pressed back in a snarl. Hugh cringed in fear.

"What in hell did you think you were doing taking the boy on survey? He's delirious. He's dehydrated and he's probably been stung. This isn't a place for tourists, you know."

The voice was not shouting at *him*. Hugh dared to look up. Hartmann Schele, hands defiantly on his hips, berated his survey team.

Joanne, who had arrived with him, acted quickly. "Water," she said. "Get some water."

In a moment she held a canteen to his lips. The water slowly soothed the fires in his head and the dreaded image of the glaring face disappeared. The sun was still overhead, flickering gently through the leaves. He was lying on the ground beside the cold stones of the well.

"There, there. Take it easy, Hugh." Joanne's voice penetrated the fog in his head and he sat up at last. He took a deep breath to collect his thoughts. What had happened? Had he fallen asleep? No, not into sleep, but into—into another place and time. He remembered bellows, screams and horrid images.

Jose helped him into a hammock where he immediately fell into a deep, dreamless sleep.

Sometime later, Joanne brought him more water. The men and Linda had gone off to work. "You really had us scared," she said. "One minute you were nodding off and the next you were screaming like a hundred baboons. In Mayan, no less."

He grinned sheepishly. "Sorry. I didn't mean to scare you. I guess you think I'm crazy."

She smiled back. "No more so than the rest of us out here. Let's not talk about this until Linda gets back. Tell me how you came to be in Yaxchilán."

He was only going to tell her the basic facts at first but then he found himself telling her everything. She listened to him and he began to trust her. He knew she would keep the conversation private. In the shaded cool grotto of the trees, Hugh told her about his unhappiness at home, his "escape" to Mexico, and about the strange feelings he'd been having since he arrived. He was too embarrassed to tell her about his nighttime escapade.

She pursed her lips. "I can see you've been under a lot of pressure. I'll try to convince Roger to help you for a few days—after all, you are his son. But Sam Sheldon is coming and you'll likely have to go back with him."

"But—"

"I can't do more than that. Here comes Linda. I won't say anything about what you've told me but now you owe us an explanation about your dream."

Hugh sighed in relief. "Thanks."

Linda brought a huge fruit in her hand. "Melon. Ripe off the vine," she said. "Here, try some."

The fruit was sweet and surprisingly cool. He felt energized.

Joanne told Linda they had been puzzling over his dream.

"Maybe you just read something," Linda suggested. "The names you were calling out were the names of Mayan rulers."

"Odd," he admitted, "but I don't know any of those people. I didn't read their names anywhere."

"Not even *Itzamna*? Or *Ix Chel*?" Linda asked. "They and God K were three of the four most powerful Mayan gods. The top god was the Sun God, *Kinich Ahau*. *Ahau* means king or great lord, *kin* means sun or day. Surely you've heard of him?"

He shook his dazed head. He wasn't sure.

"*Xibalba*? God of the Underworld? One Death and Seven Death were also underworld figures. You were hallucinating about the story of the hero twins who defeated Death in the underworld. Pretty common stuff if you know your mythology."

A tremor ran through him at the name *Xibalba*. She-ball-ba. It rang in him with resonance like the familiar sound of a pebble being dropped into the well. And *Akab d'zib*. Yes, he did know it. It meant the "Mouth of the Well." He remembered saying it. But what did it mean? Something inexplicable was going on in him, a battle for control of his own mind. He broke out in a cold sweat.

Joanne put her arm around him. "Look, we've pushed you far enough. It was a bad dream and I'm sure you must have read something you don't remember reading. This hot sun and dehydration can do funny things to people."

He decided to accept the easy explanation. "Okay. You're probably right about reading the names. But what will Jose and Schele think?"

"We'll say it was *mal turista*, a little sunstroke." She smiled. "So, that's enough of that, everyone. Back to work."

Getting back to work, though, was easier said than done. Ghostly images remained with him, haunting the periphery of his thoughts.

The others had left him for a while. But eventually Schele came over to talk to him. His hawklike features reminded Hugh of a vulture patiently waiting for something to die.

"So, you're the son of our famous Roger Falkins," he said. "I see the physical similarity now."

Hugh said nothing. He was thinking that Schele's face looked familiar, too.

"You have the strangeness, too. A most remarkable ability—to see the past."

"What do you mean?"

"Like father, like son. You both get 'feelings' about the past, do you not?"

"I can't see the past," Hugh contended. "I had a bad dream just now. You won't tell my dad, will you?"

Schele smirked. "We'll keep it our secret. No need to worry him unduly. He has a lot on his mind—like finding Bird Jaguar's unknown son."

"Is there a son?"

Schele leaned on his spade. "If he knows where the boy is, he's keeping the secret to himself. We'd all like to know. You'd want us to know, wouldn't you?"

Hugh couldn't hold up the pretence at politeness any longer. "What do you care? No one seems to believe my dad anyway. You all want to use his talent but you don't like him." He glared at the archaeologist.

"Okay. Okay. Touchy, aren't we? It's just that we need that information. I'm sure it would be to everyone's benefit to make such a monumental discovery before our time here is up."

"I don't understand."

"There's not much time, you know. Only five days. *Uayeb*. Five unlucky days."

Another warning? Hugh was sure of it. Schele's gaze was inexplicable; he had looked at him as if they might be enemies. Stranger yet was the archaeologist's cancellation of the search. He was unimpressed at the discovery of the *midden*, so with only a few days left, he said, they would have to find Bird Jaguar's phantom son somewhere else.

"Just like that man," Linda bristled when he was out of earshot. "He never comes out to do the dirty work but he's always around to criticize. The *midden* has been here for a thousand years—just think of what it could tell us."

Jose was indifferent. "He's the boss. We do what he tells us. Besides, he's right. We need conclusive proof, proof which isn't here unless it's right under our noses."

"Then why isn't he here to help us?" she retorted, her earrings jangling in the sunlight.

Hugh found her fury refreshing and amusing. She reminded him of his mother—without the punk hair—trying to stand up to the stone wall of his father when he'd made up his mind. David against Goliath. He asked her where Schele went when he wasn't with them.

"Who knows? Off on his own, though I've seen him with Garcia a lot. In fact, the survey team doesn't often work together. Jose and I often take separate trips with Mayan workmen."

"She can't trust herself to withstand my charms," Jose joked.

At that moment, Joanne came running across the field, waving her arms excitedly. "Look!" She pulled up, breathing heavily, and held out a small, carved rock to them. "I was getting some water from the well and when I leaned over to pull up the bucket, there it was. I pried it out of the wall."

"What does it say?" Jose held the carved face of the rock up to the light.

Hugh could make nothing of it.

"It's the glyph for water," she said. "But you'll have to see the rest." She led them back to the well. Schele had seen the commotion and joined them.

"Jose, give me your flashlight," Joanne said. She took the light and leaned over the well, playing the light against the rocks. "There, look at that."

Hugh narrowed his eyes to get used to the near dark. Then suddenly the algae-covered wall blazed in row after row of intricate carvings. Each rock, the size of two of his fists, was carved with the sure hand of an ancient carver, each one a story that linked all of them together into a picture of the past.

Joanne's words trembled on her lips. "*U cab*, in the land of Bird Jaguar. Nine-sixteen-five-zero-zero. That's a date. About 790 BC. And, hey, this is strange, the glyph for Lady Te-Xoc."

"Impossible!" Schele exploded. "Here, let me see." In his excitement, he practically hung upside down while Hugh and Jose held his legs. When he straightened up, his face was red.

"What is it?" Linda prompted.

Hartmann Schele stood as if he was looking into the deep past. For a moment he appeared not to have heard the question. Then he shrugged his shoulders. "False alarm. It's nothing."

"But—" Joanne began.

"Undoubtedly these stones were taken from the ruins down below and used to make the well. Hence the presence of Te-Xoc's glyph. Commoners wouldn't have used carved stones for the making of a well; they're sacred. Besides, we can't start taking apart the villagers' well—we'd have a war on our hands."

His arguments sounded reasonable to Hugh but he could see that the others looked crestfallen. Joanne was surly.

"Look," Schele decided, "it's getting late. We'd better pack up and go back."

"I'm coming back tomorrow," Joanne persisted. "You can tell your staff what to do, Hartmann, but not me. I'm going to look into this further."

Schele glared at her and, for a moment, Hugh thought he was going to hit her. But the big man backed away. "Suit yourself, Miss Nielsen," he said gruffly. "We have other work to do."

"Who was Lady Te-Xoc?" Hugh asked. They were on their way back to the camp.

Joanne had calmed down. "There was a Te-Xoc who was an ancestor of Bird Jaguar's on his mother's side," she mused, "but I think the glyph I found was a younger woman's, possibly a similarly named minor wife of Bird Jaguar's."

"But couldn't she be a link to this Bird Jaguar son that everyone is looking for?"

"That's what I'm going to try to find out tomorrow. The link is pretty weak but I don't want Schele telling me what I can or can't do."

She was determined and Hugh realized the woman was tougher than he had imagined.

He said, "It's unfair. My father could order Schele to take out those stones."

She sighed deeply. "No, Hugh. Schele's right on two counts. First, there's no relationship or connection between the stones and the ruins. They're not in any order, so it's like taking a brick from the pyramids and a brick from your house in Seattle and saying they were made at the same time. Second, we really would need to get permission from the headman of the village to take apart the wellstones. Not very likely I think."

He grinned. "How do you know our house in Seattle is made of brick?"

"Is it?"

"I think you know that."

She blushed. "I've...visited...your father from time to time. We are friends, you know."

"Good friends?"

She said finally, "You'll make a good archaeologist. You ask a lot of questions and you're persistent."

They walked in silence for a while. Hugh liked her and he trusted her but the thought of an intimate relationship between her and his father was disturbing. He still thought of his mother, his father, and himself as close-knit. He still hoped they would be a family again.

They were nearing the camp and the sun had already dipped toward the horizon. "You could talk to my father, couldn't you? Tell him to hold off sending me back? I'd like to stay."

She stopped suddenly and gave him a stiff look. "Hugh, I've done what I can. I asked him once already and I promised not to say anything about the episode this afternoon. That's all I can do for you."

"But he likes you. I know it."

"He's your father. And I'm not your mother."

He was hurt—all his hopes suddenly crushed. Joanne couldn't—wouldn't—help. He was angry, too.

Her voice softened. "You're so much alike, the two of you. He told me you were born on the same day. The Day of the Falcon."

He quelled the emotion in his voice. “Yes. Our family’s heritage is English. Norman actually. We’re descended from Sir Richard de Guise whose coat of arms was a falcon.” He showed her his signet ring bearing the profile of a falcon. “That’s how we got the name Falkins.”

“Not unlike the Mayans,” she said. “The gods decided your birth and your name. They were your fate and there was nothing you could do to alter it. No one escaped the gods, not even Blood Jaguar.”

“How’s that?

“His sign says he was condemned to die on the day of his birth.”

Hugh felt the skin on his neck tingling. “When was that?” he asked in the calmest voice he could muster.

“Three days from now.”

He was glad to return to the civilizing atmosphere of the camp, away from ghostly dreams, unlucky days and demanding presences. It was an illusion, of course. He knew he couldn’t run away from what was inside his head.

The archaeologists wanted to put their hard day behind them, too. After supper, they told stories that had them all laughing. His father puffed contentedly on his pipe and even Schele demonstrated a softer side Hugh had never seen. All that, he discovered, was illusion, too.

He was loathe to leave the campfire and head back to his tent and the dark territory of his mind. He needed company, so he offered to help Mitch with the dishes.

Mitch’s eyes darted back and forth, never looking directly into his. She rambled on about trivial things until he stopped her.

“Hey, what’s bugging you? Did I say something wrong again?” He tried to make his voice soft and concerned.

She snapped her dishtowel at a small lizard creeping across the table, causing it to scurry away into the dark. She looked at him sheepishly. “No, I did. I’m sorry I said those nasty things about your father—and about you yesterday. Joanne says you’re an all right guy.”

“She’s nice.”

“Everyone has their nice side but this place gets us down, too. I’ll be glad to get out.”

“I’ve almost forgotten what it’s like,” he agreed. “And I’ve only been here a couple of days.”

"It grows on you. You forget about the outside world. It's like you've stepped into a place where time doesn't exist."

"Yeah."

"McDonald's."

"What?" He was startled.

"I'd die for a juicy Big Mac with fries and a ton of goop."

Hugh smacked his lips. "With a strawberry milkshake."

"Supremo Pizza with olives, anchovies, jalapenos, onions, peppers…"

"A mittful of Oreo cookies."

She sighed. "Oreo cookies…"

They were silent for a few moments, each lost in thought.

"Fathers!" Hugh finally said and she exploded with laughter.

"Drawn and quartered."

"Hung and whipped."

"Shipwrecked."

"Home." He said quietly. He hadn't meant to say it but the meaning hung between them like the moon that floated placidly in the sky. This time the silence was awkward.

"Can you keep a secret?" Mitch asked. She gripped the dishtowel tightly in her hands, her eyes glancing furtively at the archaeologists who were just out of hearing distance.

"Sure."

"I mean it. There's something funny going on here."

He guffawed loudly. "No kidding. Mayan ghosts. A prowling jaguar. A boy-king who may or may not exist. This isn't exactly Normalville, is it?"

But she was serious. He could see the worry in her face. "Okay. Sorry. What gives?"

"Well," she started slowly, "there have been secret meetings at night."

He almost dropped the plate in his hand, recovering quickly. "Oh?"

"At first I thought it was—you know—lovers."

"But it wasn't."

"I don't think so. For three nights, I've tried to follow them. Last night, I finally managed to get close but there was a—a noise and suddenly they started running and I—"

"—ran into someone," he finished. His heart was racing. "It was me."

"You?"

"Yeah. You gave me a heck of an uppercut." He fingered his chin.

"You? Oh, man, I'm sorry. I was so spooked I lashed out instinctively."

"I followed them too," he added, "but I thought they might be soldiers."

She eyed him speculatively. "Did you see—um—anything else?"

He couldn't hold back the truth. "You mean the ghost? Damn near scared the life out of me."

She released a breath of pent up air. "Then I'm not dreaming after all. I nearly wet my pants."

They laughed aloud at the thought of running like scared rabbits.

She said, "You know, the accidents to the workmen, the equipment lost, even the jaguar—it's as if someone's deliberately trying to get rid of us."

"I heard them talk about a deadline."

"What could that be?"

His thoughts were turning rapidly. There were three days to Blood Jaguar's birthday and five days of *Uayeb* leading up to the end of the fifty-two year cycle when cataclysmic events were supposed to occur. But he couldn't make a connection. "Maybe it's none of our business," he said.

She looked at him decisively. "No! I think it *is* our business. In fact, we've got to do something about it."

"But what?"

"Tomorrow night. I'll show you something that will convince you."

He slept soundly, dreamlessly. The day of rigorous archaeological work had taken its toll. When he awoke in the morning, his muscles were sore and he began to appreciate the comment that archaeology was ninety percent work and ten percent luck. Fortunately, Linda did not have another hard day planned.

"Schele's sending us back to look at an area we've already covered."

"Foolishness," Jose scoffed. "We won't find anything and he knows it."

"So we're going to the village instead. We'll talk to the headman there and see if we can get permission to work on the well. You'll like the village and Mitch wants to come along to pick up more food."

The village was nearly five miles away and the only way to get there was to walk. Hugh talked to Mitch on the way.

Her mother had died when she was a small girl and Matthew McVean had chosen to keep her with him as he traveled the world. She became the son he had always wanted. When he had to, McVean left her with an aunt in New York but she was mostly educated by her father and taught herself the rest. "Seat-of-the-pants learning" he had called it, and she mimicked her father's droll, studious voice. "Do the girl a world of good. Better than all this high falutin' stuff the schools teach."

Hugh thought it strange advice from an academic but said nothing.

She had also missed out on most of the so-called "normal" things teenagers did—hanging out with friends at the mall, going to the beach, going to school dances.

"Any boyfriends?" he asked cautiously.

She shook her head vigorously. "No time."

She made him painfully aware of his own unusual circumstances. Born of an English father and an American mother, his early life was as mobile as Mitch's was. When his mother insisted on some permanence for him, he had had to learn for the first time how to fit in with the others at his high school. He was never fully successful. He got reasonably good grades and he had a few friends but he knew he was a loner and he preferred it that way. Only on the field trips with his father did he feel his true passion rising. He wanted to be an archaeologist too. He was more at home in the past than in the present.

"Strange, isn't it," he said. "We're almost alike. We've got so much in common."

"Yeah."

They followed the trail, skirting the area of the wellsite. Where the road crossed a small stream over a stone bridge, they entered the valley in which the village nestled. Hugh could see its red tiled roofs and the white splash of sunlight off its adobe walls.

They called out "*Hola*!" to small girls who were driving flocks of sheep to higher pastures and to the farmers who were already at work in their cornfields. Their greetings were returned shyly.

"The *milpa* is the most important property a man has," Jose said, pointing to the cornfield. "It's usually his only way of making a living."

Hugh could see that the labor was very hard but the workers were friendly and willing to talk to them. He liked them immediately. They soon passed thatched huts with stone fences that acted both to keep out jungle predators and keep in livestock. Linda and Jose and Mitch seemed to know everyone, and while Hugh thought the local women might be scandalized by Linda's punk looks, they accepted her natural affability.

Pigs and chickens scratched for food on the dirt floors of the compounds. Cooking fires were already hard at work on the midday meals. Mitch pointed out the three stones that supported large iron pots of simmering corn.

"The three stones that support the hearth are the center of the world," she said. "Everything has a meaning. Nothing is wasted." She was proud to impart this knowledge not out of cleverness at showing off, but because she truly admired the women.

As they approached the village, bands of children ran out to greet them, the boys especially, calling out for candy. "Bom bons! Bom bons!" they shouted.

Jose spoke rapidly to them in Spanish, dispensing a few coins and the children ran off to a sweet shop.

They entered Tres Cruces by one of the three roads coming into a rough square. The village was much larger than Hugh had anticipated. Buildings of adobe formed the walls of the square. A large church plastered in pink was topped with a squat steeple that glistened in the sun.

Women in multicolored dresses walked about barefoot, balancing heavy loads on their heads, or spreading blankets on the dirt square as they prepared to sell their wares. Some had already set up backstrap looms under the shade of a giant tree, where they made fabric for clothes. Men in white shirts and pants propped themselves up against walls, watching the strangers parade down the street.

"You'd better get used to having people look at you closely," Jose warned him. "Only gods and warriors are as tall as you."

Hugh felt he was seeing how ancient Mayans might have looked. He also felt their caution. Strangers were few and far between in the village. He pulled his camera out of his pack, snapping off several photos of the market including one of two young men in green fatigues. Then he aimed at a couple of women.

Mitch suddenly slapped down his hand. "No!"

"Hey! What…?"

"Don't ever do that," she berated him. "They don't like getting their pictures taken."

"I was just taking a photo. What's the big deal?"

"She's right," Linda chided gently. "The camera is an evil eye. If you take their picture, they think you're taking their soul."

Jose lowered his voice and gestured dramatically, slashing his finger across his throat. "You bedder watch yourself, *gringo*, or else!"

He lowered the camera.

Jose had an appointment with the headman, the *curandero*, a man he described as "both local medicine man or shaman and religious priest," from whom he hoped to win approval to work on the wellsite. "He'll ask the gods to approve our tampering."

They agreed to meet near the *curandero's* home later. Mitch and Linda went off to do some personal shopping, leaving Hugh on his own.

He was content to walk through the side streets of the village. He passed an archway that looked in on a shadowy courtyard. At the far end, three women were huddled over a small fire that sent plumes of smoke into the air. Their long black hair and scarves reminded him of the three witches in *Macbeth.*

He was surprised, as he turned the corner back on to the main street, to see Jose lounging in the shade of a tree, nonchalantly it seemed, but obviously hiding. Without knowing why, he did not announce his own presence but hugged the side of the wall nearest him and waited to see what would happen. Jose was supposed to be at the *curandero's* but he was looking for someone, waiting for someone to appear, without wanting to be seen.

Minutes went by. The people of the village strolled about on their daily business. The vendors chatted with customers as a burro went by carrying a heavy load to the tune of bells around its neck. The bell in the church tower rang the half-hour. He saw the two soldiers whose picture he had taken. Then he saw Guy Garcia.

Garcia acknowledged the soldiers.

Jose watched them closely.

Garcia dressed as any villager might, with loose fitting pants and traditional white shirt. A broad-brimmed sun hat hid most of his face. Had Hugh not been looking at the soldiers, he would have passed him without recognizing him. His business, whatever it was, was conducted on the street in full view of anyone watching. He gave the soldiers a small package, shook hands with them, and with a brief nod, struck off down the road back toward the campsite.

Hugh looked for Jose but the archaeologist had gone. He pursed his lips in thought. Another puzzle to be solved in the already complex goings-on in Yaxchilán.

CHAPTER 6

Hugh asked for directions to the *curandero's* house. But he waited by a nearby stream, giving Jose lots of time to complete his task. He immersed his hand in the cold water until it was numb, wishing his mind could also be deadened to its confusion.

As he watched the water, letting its movement and its dull roar lull him, his mind wandered. He was walking down a road. On either side were peasant huts. Only the three-stoned cooking pots stirred with life. Hammocks hung sadly. There were no women going to and fro with their huge loads perched on their heads and no running, laughing children. Cornfields were deserted.

Three ravens flew up from three stones in the pathway, cursing him. Odd. Why three stones in the middle of the path? As he drew closer, he realized they weren't stones at all but skulls.

A sense of dread overcame him. The village reeked with the scent of death and the smoke of its burning huts cloaked the sky. He heard far-off screams of terror and the thump of war drums.

The bush crackled behind him.

Two soldiers sprang at him and before he could rise, one slammed his rifle butt into his shoulder. He yelled and went sprawling into the dirt. When he looked up, the two had levelled their guns at him. He broke out in a sweat as their eyes glared into his, their hands on the guns rock steady.

"Hey, c'mon guys," he started nervously. "What kind of a game is this? Let me up."

He began to rise but a boot shot out and kicked him in the side. He fell back to the ground, wincing.

"Fotographica!"

He blinked dumbly. "Photo what? What photo?"

One pulled out a vicious looking knife. He ran his finger along the blade, gesturing at Hugh with menace.

There were sudden cries as Jose and an old man broke into the clearing with Linda and Mitch close behind. The old man's face was red with fury. He yelled at the soldiers, waving at them with his hands.

They were startled at first but when they saw who it was, they backed away nervously.

Hugh was astonished. It was the old man he had followed at the camp.

One of the soldiers demanded the *fotographica* again, though with less conviction.

Jose pulled Hugh to his feet. "They know you took a picture of them. That's against the law. Give them the camera. Do it now."

A soldier threw it to the ground and smashed it to bits with the butt of his rifle. Then he straightened up, his shoulders in a proud stance. Barking a warning at Jose and the old man, the soldier and his companion marched away.

Jose was fuming. "You're lucky that we heard the yelling. Those men are dangerous."

"Now they probably won't allow us to work the well," Linda added, clenching her fists, glaring at Hugh. "We'll be lucky if they don't kick us out of Yaxchilán."

Hugh's stomach sank. He hung his head in guilt. Then a hand touched him softly on the shoulder. He looked up into the deep, calm eyes of the old man.

The old man spoke to him in Mayan in a quiet, controlled voice.

"Who is he?" he whispered to Jose.

"The *curandero*, Don Alphonso," Jose answered, "the shaman or medicine man. He seems very interested in you."

Don Alphonso smiled broadly. He said something in Spanish to Jose and waved all of them back up the trail.

"Imagine that." Linda shook her head, perplexed, though her voice still carried a touch of anger. "He says he'll carry out the ceremony to bless the well after all. We can get to work."

Jose looked puzzled. "And then he wants to do *hetzmek* for you."

"A curing ceremony?"

"No. A birth ceremony."

Hugh grumbled. "My father wants me gone. Linda and Jose are still ticked off at me. I guess I should just face the facts and go home."

"Hey. Lighten up." Mitch poked his shoulder good-naturedly. "Looks like you're going to have a birthday party."

"That's dumb. Why does the old guy want to do a birth ceremony for me? He's weird." He forced a grin.

"Spooky, anyway," Mitch said truthfully. "Sometimes he hangs around the camp. But he's like a ghost. One minute he's there; the next he's gone. The only one he talks to much is your father."

"My dad? I wonder what they're up to."

She shrugged.

Hugh shook his head. Another mystery.

He threw down the book he was reading. Snapping a cassette into the tape deck he had borrowed from Mitch, he tried to listen to some music but the wailing of Madonna and Michael Jackson was too noisy for him. He twisted in his hammock trying to get comfortable but he had no success.

Instead, he joined the group at the lunchroom table. But the atmosphere was no better. An almost palpable tension was in the air. Mitch banged her pots too loudly; McVean paced back and forth like a hungry bear. Even the usually relaxed camp doctor, John Henry, was nervous. He dropped a coffee cup, smashing it to bits. The sound was like a window shattering.

"Tomorrow's D-Day, or rather S-Day," his father said, puffing quickly at his pipe. "Sam Sheldon's coming. And he either cancels the project or gives us an extension."

Seeing the worry in his father's eyes, he realized that the archaeologists and many of the local people, too, depended on his stepfather's decision, and he flinched at the thought that he might be personally responsible for jeopardizing the whole project. Sheldon had an unforgiving temper.

It didn't help matters that Linda had confronted Schele about the wellsite in front of everyone. She demanded they start work the next day.

Schele retaliated. "What gave you the right to go behind my back? I'm director of surveys. I decide what we'll do." He pounded the table.

"Don Alphonso has agreed to bless the well. We can't lose the chance."

"Silly old man—"

Jose interrupted quickly. "And Don Alphonso thinks he can help us find Bird Jaguar's son."

The group sat upright as one.

"Then it's true?" Edith Richards asked. "There is a son. The old man knows—"

"Not exactly—"

"Then what?" Questions came at him like a rattle of hailstones.

"C'mon then," David Kelly interjected. "What exactly did he say? We have a right to know."

There were many murmurs of assent. Hugh noticed that his father was keeping silent on the matter.

Jose waved off the eager questioning. "He said there were many unknown things he could show us—you know how the old ones like to string us along. But he did say the well was a doorway to the past."

"There, Hartmann!" Linda spat out. "You can't stop us now."

"Doorway, indeed!" Schele responded contemptuously. "If the old man knows so much then why hasn't he told us before where this preposterous Blood Jaguar is? You said it yourself, Jose. He's just trying to make himself look important."

"We can't offend the local people," Jose said. "Certainly not one as important as Don Alphonso."

"I still think this is a wild goose chase."

David Kelly looked at Roger Falkins. "Well, Roger?" he asked. "It really is your call."

Hugh's father smiled. "Naturally I'd like to see if there's anything in the well. You can have one day but I don't want anyone getting up Sam Sheldon's hopes without substantial proof. Let's get some sleep. Tomorrow's a big day."

The dark bush moved. Instinctively, Hugh grabbed for Mitch's hand but she grabbed his at the same time.

"What was that?"

"Take it easy," he whispered, sweeping his flashlight beam in a wide arc through the bush, nervously expecting to see the telltale glint of two red eyes in the dark.

Nothing.

"It's gone. I think."

"I hope." She burrowed her head into his shoulder. "Maybe we shouldn't have come. I can show you later."

He deepened his voice in what he hoped was a steady, comforting tone. "No, c'mon. We've come this far. Let's go on."

He noticed, not ungratefully however, that she continued to hold on to his hand, no mean feat on the narrow jungle trail, but he wasn't letting go either. Their flashlights lit the way.

"Here!" she whispered later.

"Why are you whispering? No one's around."

"In case...Oh, you're probably right. But we'd better keep our voices down. Maybe they've got a guard."

"Or a ghost?"

She tried to look brave.

He grinned nervously in the dark. "Eat your heart out, Indiana Jones."

"What?"

"Nothing. Go ahead."

Her flashlight revealed the doorway to the temple, a gaping black hole like a broken tooth.

"No, wait! I'll go first."

The beam penetrated the blackness, illuminating a narrow corridor barely five feet high going off left and right. He had to stoop to make his way in. The air was cold, yet his skin felt clammy. Something flittered by, brushing his cheek, before he heard the telltale skittering of bats on the roof. Footsteps marked the dusty floor.

"To the right," Mitch directed.

They stepped into a wider room where the roof vaulted into the darkness. He saw nothing at first as his eyes adjusted to the dim light. Then he gave an involuntary gasp of surprise.

Eyes. Deep-set, slanted, cruel eyes. He stepped back instinctively. The eyes were made of stone. A carving, the profile of a Mayan nobleman with a flat forehead and long pointed nose, its head was covered with a flowing fall of plumes, chest protected by a vest of linked plates. He was reaching for a helmet from a woman who was adorned with necklaces and earrings.

"Shield Jaguar," Mitch said solemnly. "And his wife, Lady Xoc." Her eyes glinted. "The team found this piece a few months ago and now someone's taken it out of the temple where it was found."

"Taken it out?"

"Stolen it. It was a decorative carving in the doorframe of a temple. Not something you'd expect to disappear. See," she pointed to a thin white line, "it's been cut away."

He ran his hand along the cut. "With power tools, I'll bet. A nice neat quick job. It would only take two people to carry it."

"There's more."

He directed the light around the room. It was filled with looted valuables: more carvings, statues, bowls, even frescoes from walls.

"So someone's been stealing these things. That's what the secret meetings are all about."

"And I'll bet the deadline is when they're going to pick up this stuff."

"Let's check out the other room."

Machinery lay on the floor. Power tools, ropes. He uncovered a large square of plastic sheeting, recoiling instantly as the face of a Mayan warrior leered at him.

Mitch stifled a gasp. "It's—it's the ghost," she whispered.

He nodded. "And here's the rest of his gear." He pulled up the shield and club. "So, no ghost."

"They were just trying to scare us," Mitch complained bitterly. "That explains the ghosts that the workmen saw, too."

"They did a good job. If I'm not mistaken, here's the rest of the sound and light show." The light revealed a canister of dry ice for making smoke and filtered lights for the ghostly appearance of the warrior.

"This is awful," Hugh groaned. "Doesn't anybody know these artifacts have disappeared? Surely the archaeologists…"

Mitch sighed. "It would take a hundred archaeologists working full time to explore all the temples and buildings in Yaxchilán. Anybody could walk in here, even with a stone-cutting saw, and go undetected and unheard. And once the artifacts have been mapped and photographed or stored away, there's no immediate reason to look at them again until we pack up. Yet, I'd say someone has been very careful and selective about what he takes. These pieces are very good but they're not from the most frequently visited ruins. Maybe they've even found an unknown temple."

"Bird Jaguar's son?" The words leaped to his throat. "Is it possible?"

"Maybe. Someone knows but he's not telling."

"Who?"

She looked at him oddly.

He caught his breath. Suddenly, he knew.

She shuffled nervously. "Of course, I'm guessing. I mean—I'm not sure."

"You know," he hissed. "Say it."

"I can't. Don't push it. Let's go."

He felt the hot rush of anger sweep through him. He tightened his fists and glared at her.

"You knew all along. That's why you brought me here, didn't you?"

"No. I—"

"It's my father, isn't it?"

She looked away.

He felt helpless. It made no sense to him. Stealing antiquities upset his father terribly. He detested people like Sam Sheldon who kept their collections private instead of sharing them with others. But his father was secretive; he disappeared for long periods of time.

"I—I'm sorry, Hugh." She touched his arm lightly. "But it's better you know now than later. You can see why I didn't want to tell you without proof. You know we'll have to tell the others."

He was furious. "And why not *your* father? Why not one of the others? You've all got it in for my dad, haven't you?"

She backed away into the darkness. "No. You don't understand. I didn't want you to find out in front of the others. I was just trying to protect you."

He counted to five and waited until he calmed down. "How'd you know about this place?"

"I came up here after we saw the ghost."

"There's more than one person involved. Who else is in on the theft?"

"I don't know," she said. "But we've got to tell someone before the deadline."

He closed his eyes. It would be the end of his father's career.

Sensing his turmoil, she wrapped her arms around him and nestled her head on his chest.

He pushed her away.

Hugh watched his "fathers" shake hands. He had dreaded the moment, certain that Sam Sheldon would order him back home.

In fact, he was forgotten or ignored by both in the drama of the moment.

When the plane landed, his father ran to help Sheldon down but he had to compete with Ruben Dario, the pilot, who ran around the plane to do the same. Both men ran into each other, jostling for the unpleasant task.

His father was fawning and even submissive. He pretended to be jolly and pleased to see Sheldon and he made sure that everyone else played up to the man with a great display of handshaking and back-slapping.

Sam Sheldon was a thin figure, his skin unnaturally white compared to the rugged tan of the archaeologists. Hugh had always thought of him as a gray man—quiet, passionless, without humour—but Sheldon played up the role of the jolly benevolent benefactor to the hilt.

"Dear, dear, Roger"—he was all smiles—"when you asked me to drop in on you, you didn't say it would be from a thousand feet." The joke was feeble but it was just the right release for the tension that was thick in the air. Everyone laughed, and even Hugh felt slightly better, remembering his own shaky landing in the plane.

He shook hands with everyone; he didn't miss a beat when he got to Hugh. "So there you are. You must tell me how you like it down here in the jungle. More exciting than home, hey? Ah"—he quickly diverted his attention to Mitch before Hugh could speak—"and who's this lovely lady?" He took her hand warmly. "Perhaps this place is not so uncivilised after all."

Hugh's insides churned. What was Sheldon up to?

In spite of the steep climb to the campsite, Sheldon got right down to business. He dismissed most of the archaeologists, leaving Hugh's father and the directors—Kelly, McVean and Richards and Schele—to report. Mitch and Hugh helped supply drinks. Sheldon nodded knowingly at talks about glyphs and dates and his eyes widened at the display of pots and knives and funeral wares. When Matthew McVean displayed Lady, he quivered with intense interest.

"Now, Roger, tell me about the boy-king." His eyes flashed. His voice rose in an excited pitch. "You say you've found him?"

"No. Not exactly. But we think we're close."

"Nonsense," Schele interrupted. "I don't believe such a person exists."

If looks could kill, he received stabs in the back from the directors.

Sheldon raised his eyebrows slightly. "Oh? Dissension in the ranks, I see. Or is it just simply professional disagreement?"

Hugh's father frowned. "Naturally, Dr. Schele is skeptical. We haven't found Blood Jaguar yet but Dr. Nielsen's discovery suggests we're close. The well could be critical. We just need time."

"Yes, I understand you need time. But time is money, don't you see. My backers want results. Surely you understand that I need proof." He smiled blandly.

"A few days, Sam."

The group leaned forward collectively in anticipation. Sheldon settled back in his chair. "Tell me more about this Blood Jaguar—what vicious names they had, don't you think?—I don't know about him."

Not likely, Hugh said to himself. Sheldon was not one to be kept in the dark and he probably knew as much as the scientists themselves.

His father's eyes glazed over with excitement. "Think of it, Sam—a boy-king to rival Tutankhamen of Egypt. If we could find him…"

"Yes, yes."

His father talked at length about the importance of Yaxchilán as a trading center but he emphasized its wealth and power. Power was something Sheldon understood.

But the man smiled coyly. "A golden tomb would be nice."

"Most of the power was in the hands of Shield Jaguar the First and later his son, Bird Jaguar. They had the real wealth and fame."

David Kelly, barely restraining himself, jumped in. "And when Bird Jaguar died, his son, Shield Jaguar Two, received an enormous legacy—the gold of nearly two hundred years of rule."

The directors' attention was fixed, eager to hear more. The millionaire's eyes gleamed with fervor. Hugh's pulse raced as he remembered what Dario had said to him in the plane: Everyone wants gold. But he hadn't forgotten the warning that went with it.

"Then it's this boy, Shield Jaguar Two, that you're looking for," Sheldon concluded.

Kelly shook his head. "Chel-Te, that was his boyhood name, was apparently the end of the line. We found *his* grave. But no gold."

"Then?"

"We think there was *another* son. Bird Jaguar knew Chel-Te couldn't hold on to the empire. The other son, the one we call Blood Jaguar, must have taken the gold away for safekeeping or hidden it in Yaxchilán."

Sheldon's voice quivered. "Have you looked for hidden passages? Tombs underground?"

"We need more time, Sam. We're so close now."

"Balderdash!" Schele exploded again. "We have no evidence of a Blood Jaguar succeeding to the throne. We should have stelae, lintels and temples. We have nothing. It's time to pack up and go home."

Sheldon steepled his fingers. His brow furrowed with decision. "I don't like to waste my money on wild goose chases," he said. "You'd better show me a good reason not to pull the plug." The accountant had replaced the treasure-hunter.

Hugh's father simmered with controlled anger—Hugh recognized the hard line of his lips. He must have thought that he had sold Sheldon. But he smiled confidently as he said, "Sam. I believe I can show you that and more."

But first, there was lunch. And siesta. Hugh knew his father could be a good poker player, too. If he had a secret hand to show, he would spin out time, waiting for the right moment to convince his patron.

They toured the site—stelae, ball courts, plaza, granary and even minor temples—hooking the money man on the wonders of the ancient world. And Sheldon was hooked, no doubt about it, even if he didn't say so. Hugh knew the look.

He was proud of the way his father displayed his feeling for the Mayan world as he was excited by Sheldon's keen interest. He had almost forgotten that there existed a personal animosity between the two men.

Had almost forgotten his own dilemma.

Sheldon hadn't. They were resting in the shade of a tree below the great Temple of Hachakyum. It rose like a wall behind them. Of all the temples, it was the principal building that depicted carvings from the life of Bird Jaguar.

Sheldon took Hugh aside. "Your mother is worried about you."

Hugh said nothing. His stomach tightened.

"Can't say as I blame you, though—for running off I mean. Mexico. Jungles. The lure of gold. I know I'd be tempted…"

He kept his face impassive, not answering the offer to respond, though his mind was in turmoil.

"A father who is certainly more romantic than me. Quite a famous man is *our* Roger." He wiped the sweat from his brow. "Finding Blood Jaguar would be a real coup for the archaeology world and him. Imagine finding his temple of gold. I can see the headlines: Father and son duo discovers twelve-hundred-year-old secret."

He couldn't contain himself any longer. "What do you want?" he snapped.

"I don't want you to make a mistake."

"What mistake? What do you mean?"

"I mean that your father could lose everything if he doesn't find what he's after. They say his luck will run out soon."

He burned with anger. "He's never been wrong. You'll see."

Sheldon never took his eyes off Hugh's. "And if he is…?"

The question remained unanswered as the group continued its survey. On the Temple of Hachakyum, scenes of Bird Jaguar's life, depicted in stone, seemed to come alive on the walls. There was the king interrogating his prisoners, showing the god, K, his royal scepter, illustrating his right to succession, preparing for his vision rites; his wife, Lady Great Skull Zero holding a bundle to her chest; sacrificial victims…falling.

Hugh's mind began to cloud. He felt faint. No! He forced himself to remain calm. Not here. He couldn't afford to have another spell here. Not now. But the carvings swam before his eyes. He took a deep breath and forced himself to go on.

They were ascending a set of steps leading to an elevated plaza behind the Temple of Hachakyum when Hugh saw Sheldon fall. He felt it first, sensed the stair coming loose under the man's weight, the stone crumbling. He reached out to break the man's fall.

Sheldon cried out. The stair exploded in a shower of stone and dust as he fell off the edge past Hugh's outstretched arms and he crashed into the bush at the foot of the stairs.

The others ran to help him, pulling him to a sitting position but Sheldon writhed in agony, holding his ankle. His forehead broke out in beads of sweat and he gritted his teeth to keep from crying out again.

"Help him up."

"Raise his leg."

"Someone go get John Henry."

"Did anyone see what happened?"

Hugh's father hovered over his sponsor like a nervous mother over a hurt child. "Sam, are you okay? We've gone to get help. What happened?"

Sheldon grimaced. "I—"

"I can't believe it," Edith Richards looked shocked. She looked straight at Hugh. "I saw it all. He didn't fall. The boy pushed him down the stairs."

"No—" Sheldon began. But the pain was too much.

Hugh's father turned to him, his face livid. "I've seen enough," he said. "Of all the stupid things to do. Get out of my sight! Go! Now!"

The evening rain broke with a fierceness that hammered the tent. Trees whipped in the wind, branches slashed the air like swords. Far off, Hugh could hear the cries of the archaeologists scrambling to save their camp from the lashings of the storm.

Thunder cracked and rolled. Dark clouds dumped more rain. He could barely see across the compound now awash in rivers of mud. A lantern flickered once and crashed to the ground.

The whole world seemed to have gone mad in an instant. A corner of the canvas awning of the lunchroom broke loose, flapping like a sail on a ship. "Your fault! Your fault!" it said.

He held his head in his hands and groaned, his thoughts thrashing like a caged jaguar. Was it his fault? Did he push Sheldon? He knew he must have pushed him, wanted to push him, wanted to get back at him for saying those things.

Oblivious of the rain, he ran from the tent. Out into the blackness of the storm and the jungle.

The storm was the worst he had ever encountered. The sky vented its rage on every living thing—plant, animal and human. Rain battered the jungle, ripping off leaves, breaking whole tree limbs. A large ceiba uprooted before his very eyes like a tooth plucked by an angry dentist. He heard its scream as it toppled and crashed only yards in front of him. He struggled to keep his footing on the slippery trail. He heard animals crashing through the jungle in panic. It could have been the end of the world.

Lightning flashed. In the surreal light something ran by. A dark shadow.

He stumbled through scrub brush, reeling against the onslaught of the wind and rain. Gasping for breath, he tripped and fell to his knees again and again, only forcing himself up through sheer willpower. He could see next to nothing in front of him. His lungs ached, head pounded.

He needed shelter.

A wall loomed in front of him, a barricade against the wind where he was able to catch his breath. But there was no protection from the rain. It continued to crash down in torrents. Burrowing under a thick bush as close to the wall as possible, he waited for the storm to stop.

When it finally did come to an end, a gusty wind continued to tear at the clouds, exposing a ragged moon. In the distance, lightning flashed and seconds later he heard the crack of thunder, but the worst was over. Water sluiced around him in small rivulets and dripped off the trees.

Only the pitiful moonlight illuminated the bush around him. A strange *feeling* rippled through him, one he had encountered before. The jaguar was waiting in the shadows.

"I know you're out there," he whispered. His voice was foggy, coarse.

No answer, but he knew. And now he could smell it too—a primitive, feral smell, pungent and familiar. He saw the two red dots of its eyes in the darkness.

He rose slowly to his feet, backing away along the wall, careful not to make any sudden movements.

It roared. And moved.

Hugh yelled instinctively, ran, all rational thought gone, as he stumbled around the wall and into the jungle. His breath came in torn rags. Leaves and branches slapped and slashed at his face. Behind him he heard the jaguar's growl and smelled its nearness.

Suddenly, it appeared in front of him. It forced him to turn back and flee the way he'd come. No matter which way he went, it had an uncanny ability to slip through the jungle ahead of him, trapping him, toying with him.

Then he slammed into the wall again. Fell hard. Air exploded out of his lungs and his head rang with sharp, intense pain. Lights flashed in front of his eyes. He looked up.

In the moonlight, the cat crept slowly toward him, deliberately, confidently, stopping within a few paces of his feet. Sleek, spotted, dangerous, its throat rumbling in low thunder, it scrutinized him carefully but made no menacing moves.

In that moment, he was back in the *zocalo*, remembering how the cat's mind reached out to touch his. His fear subsided. He admired the powerful lines of the jaguar and he began to speak to it.

His sense, born of another, more ancient Hugh Falkins, leaped across the short space between them but there were no bars this time. He knew that the jaguar was more than skin and bones. It was a spirit that roamed between two worlds, the world he was in now, and another that wavered like thin gauze just out of reach.

It walked away from him to the wall and jumped up on it.

"The wall!" he cried aloud. What had seemed to him to be an enormous wall in the hallucinatory effects of the storm was only a low-lying mound about four feet high. It lay on its side, cracked in several places. He rose and went to it, scraping away some of the leaf mold and dirt covering it.

Now he knew. The moonlight revealed a stela, a stone pillar, carved with intricate Mayan carvings. And predominating the pillar was a face, the face of a being that was half-man, half-jaguar.

Blood Jaguar!

They found him by mid-morning, lying by the stela, dirty and wet, sleeping soundly, but otherwise unhurt. Mitch found him. She held him in her arms, cradling him, talking wildly in his ear, worry etched on her face. And she was crying.

"Why did you leave, Hugh? Where did you go?"

His father pulled him to his feet and hugged him. "Thank goodness, you're all right. You scared us half to death. We've been up all night looking for you in this storm."

Joanne poured a cup of hot coffee for him. "Here, have some of this," she ordered.

His hands trembled as he held the cup. The hot liquid shot through him like adrenaline. He sputtered and his eyes watered but he drank the whole cupful.

"I'm sorry," he finally said. "I—I wasn't thinking. I didn't think anyone would care if I disappeared off the face of the earth."

"You were angry," his father conceded. "With good reason. Edith thought she saw you push Sam Sheldon down the stairs and we—I—thought so, too. But that Sheldon's a tough old bird. He only hurt his ankle. And when we shipped him back to Villahermosa, he told us that he had just slipped. Said it wasn't your fault. Damn, I'm sorry for accusing you."

"I was beginning to wonder if I really did."

Joanne scowled. "Well, I *would* have pushed that old toad. I don't like him."

His father allowed himself a small chuckle. "Agreed. But before he left, Sam gave us five more days to come up with something."

"How about this?" Mitch shouted. She pointed at the stela.

"Oh—" Joanne exclaimed. Her lips began to tremble with excitement. "Look, Roger! It's incredible!"

Hugh's father was already pulling leaf mold off the stonework and rubbing his hands gleefully over the carvings. "This it is!" he yelled. "No doubt about it!" He grabbed all of them in an enormous bear hug. "We found him—Blood Jaguar!"

"Hugh found him," Mitch said proudly.

"Yes," his father agreed. "Hugh Falkins, discoverer of the lost boy-king of the Mayans."

Joanne wagged her finger. "Not yet. This is just a clue. But as you said, Roger, we've got five days to find the real thing. So let's get cracking."

"Where are the workmen?" Hugh's father asked the archaeologists upon his arrival back at camp. "We've got things to do."

David Kelly looked peeved. He ran his hand through his thin white hair. "They've gone."

"Gone?"

"Disappeared. Skeddadled. The storm scared them off."

"But it's over now," Hugh interrupted. "Surely, they'll come back."

"There's more to it than that, I'm afraid. They say that the storm was no ordinary storm. They think the Mayan gods are angry with us."

The Mexican archaeologists, even the usually talkative Garcia, were quiet and restless. Their eyes darted furtively as if something dire could happen at any moment.

"Posh!" Edith Richards declared. "Silliness. This is the twentieth century."

Oliver interjected nervously, "No. It's true. It's the end of the Mayan year. It is also the end of the *tun*, the cycle of years. They believe something very important and catastrophic is about to happen."

Hugh wondered if Oliver didn't half believe the stories himself.

"We'll see about that," his father said coldly. "The story about a man-eating jaguar is just superstition too. I talked with the workman. He never *saw* the jaguar. He'd only heard about it and he was so scared he dropped his own *machete* and cut himself."

"Nevertheless..." Oliver began.

"I'll talk to Don Alphonso. But first—" He told them of the discovery of the stela. It was like sending a charge of electricity through them—they all wanted to see it immediately. Hugh's disappearance was mostly forgotten in the ensuing excitement but Edith Richards fussed over him saying how sorry she was to have made the mistake.

His father calmed them down. "First things first. We've got to get this place back to normal."

All of the tents were down, the lunchroom was leaning at a perilous angle and the compound was littered with downed trees and leaves. David Kelly issued orders like a battlefield general, sending his troops off to clean up the mess.

Hugh changed into dry clothes and helped re-erect the lunchroom so there was a dry, sheltered area under which Mitch could rearrange her kitchen.

The sun came out, hot as usual, but it dried the rain-soaked camp quickly. By siesta, his soggy tent was back up and most of the camp was back in operation.

Then the *curandero* arrived.

CHAPTER 7

The *curandero's* face was wrinkled, his hair grayed and his shoulders slightly stooped. Baggy Mexican peasant's clothes hung on him like a scarecrow's but he had an aura of power and decisiveness. His eyes were expansive, deep, searching.

Hugh's father welcomed him warmly and Hugh saw that the two men were obviously great friends. "Don Alphonso, *Jefe*," he said, "honors us with his presence. We welcome the headman and his two priests."

Mitch provided lunch for the guests and when they were ready, the small party proceeded back up the hill to the wellsite.

Jose explained that the well was the source of water for the villagers, the source of life. It was protected by Chac, the God of Rain, and his attendants. His peace could not be upset without the appropriate prayers and rituals. Don Alfonso and his priests set small fires at each of the four cardinal points of the compass around the well. On them were placed votive offerings. Each of the watchers had brought four small items that they placed on each fire, a symbolic sacrifice to each of the four gods who sat at the four points of the world. At each, Don Alfonso prayed in ancient Mayan.

"He says that the well is the mouth of darkness," Jose translated. "*Akab d'zib* is the entrance to the underground world, the underworld river which runs beneath our feet leading to the chambers of *Xibalba.* To enter is to penetrate into a sacred opening when time changes and all the evil things there can rise up to the surface world. Only by satisfying Chac with sacrifices can this be prevented."

Hugh was awed by the sense of mystery and he felt a sense of rightness about the ceremony. But the images in his dizzy spell also came back to him briefly, warning him of danger from the well.

Don Alfonso called for a chicken from one of his priests. He held the squawking bird above the well itself, intoning ancient words, and then, taking a knife from his assistant, slit the chicken's throat. Blood gushed from the wound, splattering his hands and face. The chicken squawked in agony, once, then died. He shook the blood over the well and then with a final flourish, threw the chicken down the wellshaft. The sacrifice was on its way to *Xibalba,* the Underworld.

Hugh released his breath, unaware until then that he had been holding it. He wet his dry lips and wiped his brow.

The ceremony was over. Before she left, Mitch gave Hugh a little wave of her hand, silently mouthing "see me later." Don Alphonso and his priests left, their job done. Hugh's father took a team up to examine Blood Jaguar's stela, leaving Joanne, Linda, Jose and Hugh at the well. Schele grumpily dismissed the whole affair and stomped away.

Hugh and Jose strung a set of battery-operated lights down the well. Like Christmas tree lights, one was set every five feet to a depth of thirty feet. An aluminium ladder led down to the water's surface, six feet below.

Joanne suited up in scuba gear. "This whole exercise could be a bust," she cautioned the others. "Maybe there's nothing there at all."

"It's worth a try," Linda urged her. "I'd like to find something of value. Anything to put that pompous primate, Schele, in his place."

Hugh agreed. He was excited about the prospect of discovery and, scientific advancement aside, his mind *was* filled with tales of ancient maidens covered in gold, offerings sacrificed on bloody altars and tribute thrown into the well of sacrifice.

Joanne must have guessed what he was thinking, for she punched him playfully. "Don't get your hopes up. I'm not a virgin and I don't intend to get sacrificed. It's the glyphs I'm really after. If I'm right, this whole area was once a village with a small temple. Maybe Blood Jaguar's."

They watched her eagerly as she heaved herself up on to the rim of the wide well. Linda's eyes were intent. Jose bit his lip nervously. Hugh quivered in anticipation. He wished he were going down. He had just learned to scuba dive himself.

When the lights were switched on the pool erupted in yellowish light. Joanne descended the ladder to the water's surface and slipped in. She put on flippers, adjusted the mouthpiece, turned on an underwater flashlight, and gave them the thumbs up sign. Then, with a wave, she upended and dove down.

They followed the trail of her bubbles that rose to the surface with dull popping sounds. "We'll give her twenty minutes," Linda reminded them, "then we'll flash the lights off and on as a signal to come back up."

To pass the time, Hugh asked Jose about Don Alphonso.

Jose looked thoughtful. "He's a very strange man. His knowledge of the history of the area is incredible—you'd almost think he lived for hundreds of years. He's the most respected headman for miles and miles but he's also a revered shaman. They say he can perform miracles."

"What was that thing he was supposed to do on me?" Hugh asked.

"The *hetzmek*?"

"Yeah."

Jose scratched his head. "Very strange, that. It's generally a ceremony to commemorate the birth of a new child or a young person's coming-of-age into manhood. But why Don Alfonso would want to do one for a foreigner is a mystery to me."

"Twenty minutes are up," Linda declared. She flicked the lights off and on three times.

They waited expectantly.

"Hey! Something's wrong," Hugh noticed. "There aren't any bubbles. There should be bubbles from her regulator."

All three craned over the lip of the well to see. The surface was placid.

"My god!" Linda squeaked. "What can we do?" She flicked the lights on and off again, desperately.

"Maybe she passed out," Jose said. "I can't swim."

"And I can't scuba dive."

Hugh was already kicking off his runners. "I can. Give me that extra snorkel and mask." There was no hesitating now. They all sensed the urgency.

"Be careful," Linda urged.

Hugh plunged into the water. The sudden cold of the water was so shocking he almost swallowed a mouthful but he quickly surfaced to fix the mask and snorkel to his face. Then he twisted his body into a downward dive following the row of lights. With powerful strokes he shot toward the bottom. Carved, wavering faces stared at him as he descended. His head pounded with the beating of his own heart and the pressure on his ears increased. His lungs hurt, yet he went on, squinting into the darkness, hoping to see something.

He couldn't see Joanne, though the water was surprisingly clear. He'd have to go back soon; his lungs couldn't take much more. Then something grabbed at him. Something cold and strong. He wrestled to free himself from its grip but it was too late. It had him by the waist and pulled him down.

The force slammed him against the wall of the well, jarring the mask, and the lights went crazy. He flailed for purchase, panicked and was swept away into the darkness.

He struggled against the current and when his lungs could finally take no more, he involuntarily gasped for air. He expected water to rush into his mouth but suddenly he was *breathing!* And he *heard* the passage of water as it slapped against stone.

Shuttling down the tunnel with his head just above the surface, he tried to control his movement. But he slammed his shoulder against an outcrop of rock and cried out.

"Here!" A voice called in the darkness.

"Wha—?" He hit the rock again and was pinned against it. Light flashed into his eyes.

"Hugh. Here, grab my arm."

Joanne was perched on a bench of rock jutting out into the stream, one hand on an underwater flashlight. Her strong hands reached down and dragged him, coughing and sputtering, onto the ledge.

For an eternity, he gasped for air. Then he began to breathe regularly and the pounding in his head stopped. "Thanks."

"You shouldn't have come after me, Hugh. We're in a fine mess now."

"Where are we?"

"An underground river." She flashed her light around the tunnel. The roof was only a couple of feet over their heads, the river a black terrifying torrent. "It feeds the wellsite. But it's too strong to swim back upriver. We'll have to go down."

"No. No. We'll die." He started to panic, his voice echoing like a gunshot in the small cavern.

Joanne shook him. "Settle down! Listen to me! It's going to start raining soon. When that happens, the river will overflow." She played her light up to the roof. "See how wet it is? The river's at its slowest now so we'll have to go. You have to do it."

He took a deep breath. "Sorry, I just flipped for a moment."

"We'll use our snorkels to breathe. I can't take the tanks in case they jam against the rocks."

He forced himself to calm down. They linked their arms around each other's waists.

"Sure you'll be okay?"

"No choice, is there?" He breathed slowly, psyching himself up for the ordeal ahead. "Whenever you're ready."

She squeezed him tightly. "Let's go."

The next moments were a blur. He sensed only his desperation to cling to Joanne and to suck air into his burning lungs. They were banged and battered against the walls of the stream for what seemed like hours but was probably only seconds. And then they were suddenly ejected out of the stream into mid-air and they fell a long way before plunging into a pool far below.

Water swirled madly. Light flashed. Voices yelled. He felt a vice grab on to his ankle and he was unceremoniously pulled to the shore.

"Give her mouth-to-mouth. I'll help Hugh," someone said.

He felt his chest being squeezed and he coughed up water. He retched again and again until the water was gone. Finally he blinked his eyes and looked at his surroundings.

Sunlight streamed through a fissure in a huge cavern, lighting the floor where he sat. Forty feet above him, tree roots broke through the cavern roof and hung like stalactites. Halfway up the cavern wall, the underground river spat out in a curving fall to the pool below before it disappeared into a black vortex at the far end of the cavern.

His father smiled in relief. "Nice of you to drop in. This is the second time I've had to rescue you in one day. You sure get yourself into some sticky messes, don't you?"

He grinned sheepishly. "Where are we, Dad?"

"Roger, what on earth…?"

Joanne was beginning to look around her, her voice sharp with surprise and awe.

"You mean 'what *in* earth,' don't you?" he laughed mischievously. "David, I guess we'll have to tell them our secret now."

Kelly chuckled amiably. "We will. But first, do you mind telling us where *you* came from? I just about died of shock when I saw you coming out of the air."

Joanne explained how the underground river went right under the wellsite.

"Linda and Jose!" Hugh exclaimed. "They'll be going crazy. They'll think we've drowned."

"Give me your radio, Roger," Joanne said. "I'll call them."

"Not if you don't want to give them a heart attack first. They'll think you're a ghost. I'll do it."

His father went back up to the surface to call. They were less than half a mile from the wellsite and just above the terraces on which the Mayan temples had been built. Ten minutes and several explanations later, he said, "I told Sam Sheldon I'd have something pretty spectacular for him and here it is."

He pulled back a plastic sheet covering an excavated archaeological pit. Protruding from the ground were masses of bones and skulls piled in a heap. And among them, glinting in the feeble sunlight, was gold!

Hugh knelt beside the pit, his eyes wide with surprise while the others exclaimed their own amazement. There were gold pendants, chains, plates and other objects, scattered like debris on a junk heap.

"Sacrifice," David Kelly said. "The accumulation of hundreds of years of human sacrifice and gold to placate the gods."

"Thrown into the well," Joanne guessed.

"Exactly. We think this cavern was once a *cenote* or underground well. See up there, above the waterfall?" He pointed. "That's a platform, likely where the sacrifices took place. The victims were then thrown into this pool."

"And the way the bones are piled in a kind of curved bed," Hugh's father continued, "suggests that some of the bodies floated into this little back pool and sunk into the silt instead of being carried on."

"Amazing!" Jose said sincerely. "A national treasure."

"How did you find it?" Hugh asked.

"Don Alphonso led us to it. He knew we'd find it sooner or later. And he trusts us to do the right thing with it."

"But—but why didn't you say anything to us before?" Linda asked petulantly. "Why the big secret?"

Hugh's father took out his pipe. "Two reasons. One, we knew we might need a big surprise to convince Sam Sheldon to continue to sponsor us. We couldn't afford to let that information out over the airwaves to him or we'd have every treasure hunter in the world down on us."

"You mean he'd leak the secret?" Hugh asked.

"I mean that *someone* would." The smoke from the pipe curled slowly into the air. "Now, I want you all to keep another secret," he said solemnly. "We said nothing about this location to keep it safe from thieves who've been regularly stealing antiquities from Yaxchilán."

He could have dropped a thunderbolt on them. They couldn't believe there was a thief in their own group.

"Well, thieves or no thieves," Joanne concluded, "we can't keep this discovery from the others. Not now."

"You're right. They deserve to see it. We'll have to post a guard here all the time from now on. We'll monitor all calls that go out of the camp and watch all unusual activity."

Hugh was relieved that his father could not have been a thief himself. But he'd have to tell Mitch to keep their secret. Then they could lay a trap for the thieves—and catch them red-handed.

The search for Blood Jaguar's tomb went into full gear. With Don Alphonso's help, Hugh's father convinced the workers to resume work. Guards were posted at the cavern. A carefully written message went to Sam Sheldon asking him to come back as soon as possible.

Blood Jaguar's stela was tantalizing. Though only partly completed before being abandoned, its glyphs hinted at his importance; important enough, they hoped, to warrant a tomb full of riches. The whole site was scoured again for clues.

Everyone was swept up in the excitement. Even Hartmann Schele caught the buzz and he was everywhere, prodding his workers tirelessly. Joanne re-examined the wellsite walls but with the added protection of a safety harness.

Mitch apologized profusely to Hugh for suspecting his father was the antiquities thief but he realized that he was equally at fault for getting angry with her. They agreed that they'd keep their secret for the moment.

The crew searched carefully but found nothing. It was as if the boy-king was a phantom. Euphoria gave way to fatigue and disillusionment.

After three straight days, they were given a day off before Sam Sheldon was to return. Hugh knew his father was disappointed but he hoped the discovery in the cavern would satisfy Sheldon. The guards, of course, would remain vigilant.

Most of the team opted to rest but Linda said, "Let's go to Palenque town. We'll sleep in a real bed for a night. Get some real food."

"What's wrong with my food?" Mitch complained.

"Nothing, really. But just think, Mitch—duck à l'orange, filet mignon, prime rib. No dishes..."

Mitch groaned. "Say no more. A day off cooking's fine with me."

"We can go by river. It'll be faster and more fun."

In the end, Hugh, Mitch, Linda and Jose were the only ones to go.

Seen from a plane, Hugh remembered the Rio Usumascinta as a glittering snake winding through the jungle, but that image was dashed as their motor launch plunged through wild waves and narrow canyons through beautiful, placid stretches and swamps. On their right, the territory they were passing was the state of Guatemala, the river forming its natural and political boundary.

Waves crashed against the launch. The sky flashed by. He could see the white peaks of the ruins above the undisturbed jungle, recalling that the river had once been the main route for trade for the Mayans for hundreds of miles.

He marveled at the wildlife that came to the river's edge. Howler monkeys, like black furry balls, hung in the fruit trees draping over the water. A flight of colorful toucans flittered overhead. A huge silvery hawk dipped into the river and emerged with an enormous fish in its talons.

The nearest town, Frontera Echeverria, forty-five minutes downriver, was small, a starting point for occasional travellers who went to Yaxchilán and Bonampak. The four didn't stop but moved on through a peaceful, turgid part of the river canopied with vines and bromeliad-laden branches thirty feet above their heads. Placid turtles and dangerous-looking crocodiles sunned themselves on the muddy banks, blue and gray herons ghosted the shallows, and otters, hawks and kingfishers played along the shoreline.

They passed small cooperatives, colonies of houses and stores occupied on the Mexican side by refugee groups, stopping at one for lunch. Hugh's height was an amusing sight to the tousled, barefoot children who emerged from a single-room thatched school. The visitors were invited to eat a simple meal of *tortillas* and *frijoles*, corn cakes and beans.

Jose asked whether there was any trouble from the army. No, everything was *muy tranquilo,* one man said. Once in a while the

Mexican army would arrive unexpectedly to search for guerrilla soldiers from Guatemala crossing the border. But now all was very quiet.

Hugh sensed Jose's doubt. He didn't know much about the political situation but he knew that the shadowy jungle hid more secrets than any of them could know.

They spent the night in the town of Santo Domingo Palenque and, true to Linda's predictions, slept in beds, had hot showers and gorged like pigs in a local hotel. Even Mitch agreed it was better than her cooking.

The next morning they headed out very early to visit the Mayan ruins at Palenque. The ancient buildings were wreathed in mist and Hugh felt as if he had walked into the past. A friend of Jose's, Mateo Enrique, accompanied them as an official guide.

"The jewel in the Maya kingdom," Mateo said with a flourish of his arms, but Hugh could see that for himself. He gazed with awe at the hundred-foot high Temple of Inscriptions, the resting place of King Pacal the Great. To his left a wide stairway led down to the palace where Palenque kings and queens had been buried for centuries. And above them, in an amphitheater ringed by steep hills, sat the three temples of Chan Bahlum, Pacal's son.

"We'll start with Shield Pacal," Mateo said. "The king who ruled from 615 to 683 AD. He was nearly eighty when he built this temple. But what a temple!"

They ascended the steps and entered a dark room lit by soft electric light. On the back wall were two huge blocks of glyphs and on an inner room a third. "There are six hundred and forty glyphs altogether," he explained. "Nowhere in Mexico are there more than here, and they prove that Pacal's son, Chan Balum, was his rightful successor."

Hugh examined them closely. "It seems to me that kings had a lot of trouble making sure their sons had the right to claim the throne."

"You're right. The family of the Pacal was so large, there was a lot of internal fighting for the throne."

"Just like a soap opera," Linda chuckled.

When they descended down the stone stairway to the temple floor eighty feet below, Mateo turned on a light. He paused dramatically and launched into a prepared speech.

"When Pacal died, his laborers hollowed out the heart of a giant stone to house his body and above it they placed this pyramid. The stairwell was backfilled with tons of rock so no one would disturb his rest. In 1952, Alberto Ruz Lhullier discovered the seal. It took him and his workmen three years to remove the rubble. Ruz recorded these words: 'We had arrived at the door of mystery. Widening the opening slightly, I put the electric light through…to my amazement, out of the shadow rose a vision from a fairy tale.'"

Hugh tingled with anticipation as they entered a small doorway through which he had to stoop. Another light, a reddish, ghostly glow, filled the crypt. He was stunned. The room was filled from floor to ceiling with glistening, sculpted walls. On them, giant stone soldiers guarded the room, overseeing an enormous stone coffin with an elaborately decorated lid.

"Twelve and a half feet long, seven feet wide and ten inches thick." Mateo read Hugh's thoughts.

On it, the king was falling—floating, it seemed—between two complex tree branches.

"Didn't Eric Von Daniken suggest that Pacal was an astronaut?" Mitch asked. "It looks to me like he could be riding the controls of a spaceship."

Mateo snorted. "Nonsense! The carving shows Pacal at the moment of death as he falls from the world of the living into the underworld where he will emerge as a god." He pushed back the sarcophagus lid which slid back easily on recently installed roller bearings. "Behold the king, Shield Pacal, himself!"

The king's remains lay in state with a jade mask over his face, jade pendants in his earlobes and, over the skeleton, a red cinnabar cloth representing the color of the reborn sun. Hugh was impressed by the stately repose of the thirteen-hundred-year-old king, touched by the preparation and care that had gone into ensuring that he would enter the underworld successfully. Somewhere, he was sure, Pacal reigned in his own heaven.

Back above ground, they saw that several buses had arrived and the tourists were pouring out to see the site.

"We'll go up top to the other temples," Jose suggested. "This mob won't be up there for a while." They entered the Tomb of the Cross, Chan Balum's own building, and there they were greeted by another amazing display of hieroglyphic art. One picture in particular caught Hugh's eye. "That's the son, I guess," he said. "And here's Pacal, the father. But what's he giving him?"

"The royal scepter," Mateo said. "Proof that he is the legitimate heir to the throne."

Hugh imagined the ceremony taking place before his eyes. He could see the glittering of torchlight off the carved walls and off the shining skin of the palace guards. He could smell the heavy incense in the air, hear the low mumbles of prayer from the priests. But in his imagination, he saw Bird Jaguar, not Pacal, dressed in the rippling skins of jaguars and adorned with a headdress of colorful quetzal feathers. And watching the proceedings was another figure, a phantom, dappled by the shadows in the small room. His face was cruel, eyes narrow and searching, fists curled in silent rage and his body leaned forward as he watched the ceremony.

A priest? No, another noble, Hugh decided, one who wanted Bird Jaguar dead.

"Who is he?" he pointed, trying not to appear too eager.

The guide scrunched up his shoulders and peered down to look. "Several dignitaries were present at the ceremony. Let's see, this one wears the shell symbol, a visitor from Tulum over on the Atlantic Ocean."

Hugh stiffened. Impossible as it seemed, he knew the man.

One Shell.

"Look out!" Jose yelled.

Hugh was drowsing at the wheel of the boat on the trip back upriver. He snapped his head up just in time as a crocodile slid from the shadowy banks and arrowed toward them. The croc hit the boat with a jarring thud, knocking him back, making him lose control of the boat. Mitch and Linda screamed.

He tried to regain his balance but the boat slammed broadside into a big wave. Mitch tumbled over the side into the water. Jose lunged for her but missed and she disappeared.

The surface boiled. Mitch popped up gasping for air at the same time the crocodile veered for her flailing arms.

Hugh reacted quickly. He yanked on the wheel, turning the boat in a sharp U and revved the engine. As the dark snout slashed through the water, he aimed the prow and slammed into it.

The crocodile, stunned by the impact, stopped, giving Mitch time to grab the gunnels while Linda and Jose began pulling her up. But then it saw her. Its jaws snapped only inches behind her. Mitch screamed. Jose rose to his feet, bracing his pistol in both hands, and fired into the thrashing reptile. It roared in pain and went under in a confusion of reddish-brown water.

Linda pulled Mitch into the boat. The girl's shirt was ripped down one arm and blood ran through the ragged tears. She cried out, her face contorted in pain. Hugh gunned the engine and headed upstream, away from the dangerous shoals.

Linda grabbed a first aid kit. Expertly she bandaged Mitch's bleeding arm. "That'll do for now," she said. "At least until we get you to camp. Then John Henry can deal with your arm properly."

"Are you okay, Mitch?" Hugh wanted desperately for her to be all right.

"Yeah. Fine," she grimaced. "Teach me to go for an afternoon swim."

Jose was not so offhand. "Hugh, I should have told you to stay away from the shore. Thank goodness you were so quick. That was a smart thing to do."

He brushed aside the compliment. "Where'd you learn to shoot like that?"

"Skills of the archaeologist's trade." He shoved the pistol back in its holster. "We're almost there."

They were coming into the oxbow of the river and Hugh saw once again the temples of Yaxchilán rising bone-white from the lush green jungle. He had never approached this way before. Yet it appeared before him as familiar as his own home in Seattle. Too familiar. The last piece of the puzzle fell into place in his head with a click. The dreams. The voices. And now One Shell. It all made a weird kind of sense but he was stunned by his conclusion.

What he was thinking was impossible.

They docked at the plaza and made their way toward the camp. At midafternoon they expected the camp to be deserted but were surprised to see the archaeologists and workers standing in the center of the compound. And surrounding them were Mexican soldiers.

"Hey, what's going on here?" Linda called out. All eyes shifted her way as the small group entered the clearing.

"Dad? What—?" Hugh started.

His father's face was livid. His eyes narrowed and he clenched his fists tightly. "You could have saved yourselves a trip. We've been ordered to leave Yaxchilán."

CHAPTER 8

Lieutenant Ruiz, an unsmiling man with a thin black moustache, insisted that they were being evacuated for their own safety as there was "suspected guerrilla activity" in the area. He permitted them to take only personal items, promising they would be back in a day or two and that the camp would be safe. They would be escorted by trucks to the village.

John Henry railed at the soldiers for moving Mitch but it was useless. Hugh caught up with her in the first aid tent just before they left.

"How are you feeling?" he asked, sitting beside her.

She smiled wanly, holding up the bandaged arm. "Hurts like hell. But it's still there, thanks to you."

He tried to cheer her up. "Shucks mar'm. T'warn't nuthin'."

She leaned her head on his shoulder and sighed. "It looks like this whole project's going down the tubes. We'll be lucky if they let us come back to get our stuff."

"I'm sure it'll be okay. My father says that Don Alphonso is hopping mad and he tore a strip off of that young lieutenant."

"How did he know the army was here?"

He shrugged. "That old man seems to know everything."

"I doubt he can help, though. I'm beginning to think that the project is unlucky. Too many things have gone wrong, and just when we've found something really exciting—wham!—this happens."

"Too many things to be natural if you ask me."

Mitch sat up. "What do you mean?"

"You said yourself that things have been going wrong since day one—accidents, a ghost scare, the loss of the workmen. Pretty convenient, don't you think, if the person who stole those antiquities wanted them out of here tonight."

"You think this evacuation was planned to get us out of the way?"

"Possibly."

"Wow." She was silent a moment. "Then who? We still don't know."

He stood up. "Time to go. I can hear them calling. Look. I'm going to get to the bottom of this, so help me." He told her his plan.

Mitch rose in concern, though the sudden movement made her wince. "Don't do anything foolish. The thieves could be dangerous."

"Don't worry."

He was sure the evacuation was a trick. With everyone out of the camp, the thieves would have a clear opportunity to take the remaining antiquities. No doubt the army was in on it, too. He planned to photograph the theft but he'd have to escape first.

Soldiers were everywhere and each one seemed to be given the job of guarding a camp member. The boy who guarded Hugh could not be more than a year older than him but the submachine gun in his hands gave him a clear air of superiority. Hugh wondered if he could be as determined-looking himself if he had been in the U.S. Marine Corps.

He'd have to make his move now. They were being led to a large army truck covered in camouflage green. He motioned to his guard that he wanted to use the *lavatorio* and the young man nodded indifferently. But Edith Richards chose that moment to start complaining to him about the unfairness of it all.

"What's going to happen to all the artifacts, especially the gold ones? That's what I want to know," she rattled on. "Likely as not they'll disappear."

"These men look pretty serious," David Kelly took up the argument. "If there is a war, Edith, we don't want to be caught in the crossfire."

Hugh held in his frustration. The conversation had already drawn the attention of soldiers. Now he wouldn't be able to slip away. Lieutenant Ruiz shouted an order for them to be ushered toward two trucks. He glanced around desperately. "I'll sit in the other truck with my dad," he said loudly to David Kelly, making sure that both he and Edith would hear. As he hoped, they barely acknowledged him.

When he sauntered over to the second truck he made sure to let the others know he'd go in the first truck. His timing had to be perfect. He watched until the guard let him go, assuming he got in the truck. Then, just as the first truck began to pull away, he slipped alongside, using it as a blind and darted behind a cinderblock building. He flattened himself against the wall and waited.

He was in luck. The soldiers' attention was lax as the trucks roared away in a belch of black smoke and grinding gears. He ran from the camp center, taking a circuitous route past the guards and down to the ruins.

Hugh moved quickly, for the sun was beginning to go down behind the highlands. Its light dusted the plaza with a soft glow, and he could see shimmering waves of heat rising from the stones. Darkness would soon drop like a blanket. He planned to hide out until late evening and then make his way to the temple where the stolen artifacts were stored. In the backpack the soldiers had allowed him to take, he had brought a flashlight, mosquito lotion, jacket and the camera he borrowed from Mitch.

A storeroom off the plaza made an excellent hideaway. Its high vaulted ceiling with a small opening through which air entered made it cool and dry. Finding no snakes, he lay down and tried to get some rest.

The rain woke him. It crashed against the stones, gushing down across the plaza where more than a millennium ago Mayan kings and queens had walked. When it stopped, he set out, glancing at the luminous dial of his wristwatch. Nearly ten o'clock. Even in the dark, he knew his way. His sneakers sounded unnaturally loud on the wet stones so he walked carefully so as not to alert the soldiers.

At the west end of the plaza, he made his way across the ball courts. He could have been home watching TV or doing his homework, maybe hanging around somewhere with a gang of friends, he thought with some amusement, but instead he was sneaking through a Mayan ball court of the eighth century on his way to uncover an antiquities heist. His light-heartedness passed quickly and the queasy feeling he'd had earlier in these same ruins returned. He felt the stares of hundreds of people looking down on him. A dull roaring echoed in his head. He shook it off. He couldn't be concerned with the strange feelings now—he had things to do. Yet, when he left the ball court, the roaring stopped.

He approached the camp carefully, looking for possible danger. Thinking it deserted, he started forward until the brief red glow of a cigarette pulsed in the darkness and the wind brought a whiff of its thick smoke.

He allowed himself a silent smile. If the soldier's position was so easily given away, security was relaxed; he'd walk right by them. So it was that he almost walked carelessly right into a second guard. Only at the last moment did he suddenly stop, when the hidden soldier coughed gently, giving away his location. Hugh tensed, holding his breath, then slid quietly behind a tent. He heard voices. The captain of the guard doing his rounds. Three of them then. How many more?

He tripped over a tent rope in the darkness, and fell heavily to the ground. The *twang* seemed as loud as the crack of a whip to him but no one turned around. Letting out a big breath, he backed away, slowly, quietly, until he was safely past them.

The slope was lit by narrow shafts of moonlight that sifted through the clouds. When he reached the temple, he headed toward the entrance, then stopped. He'd be trapped inside. Better look elsewhere. A niche between the sidewall of the building and a ceiba tree root that clutched the stonework provided a better hiding spot. Lathering on insect repellent, he draped the dark jacket over his head and settled back to wait.

The night was alive with sound. Parrots chattered from the treetop, frogs croaked in the undergrowth, and rainwater dripped from trees, gushing down the hillside in rivulets. There were strange sounds too, sounds he tried to identify but couldn't. *Trill. Gargle. Grunt. Bark.* Sometime later, something large crashed through the jungle only yards away. Mosquitoes found where he was and they went after him with a vengeance. The thought of crawling things made him itchy and uncomfortable but he hunkered further into the niche and tried to ignore it.

The world exploded.

He jerked up in surprise as thunder cracked. Lightning flashed in lurid blues and greens. Staccato chattering ripped through the underbrush, metallic pounding hammered at his ears. Then, a helicopter flew directly over him, its searchlights jabbing the darkness. He understood then that the thunder was the explosions of bombs, the lightning the firing of guns. The helicopter clattered over the ruins like an angry, deadly insect.

He cringed in his cubbyhole as gunfire cracked and blazed around him.

Pain shot through his head. His eyes burned. Visions of battle flashed before his eyes. He heard men's cries, felt their fear. But the picture in his head—what had happened?—they carried knives and clubs, not guns. They wore plumed headdresses. A tall, majestic figure appeared in the dust of battle—regal, dangerous, wearing a jeweled skull headdress. He saw Hugh and his club rose…

Hugh screamed.

The blow never fell. When he looked up, the jeweled warrior had gone. The war ended as quickly, too. The helicopter doused its lights and flew off over the horizon. Intermittent yells pierced the night, eventually stopped. Sporadic light from small bush fires went out and the breeze took away the stink of the gunfire.

He sobbed. Stupid. Stupid boy, he told himself over and over. Stupid not to believe the soldiers. Stupid not to believe there really was a war. Worst was the dream—it was unnerving. It was—so real. What was the matter with him? Was he going crazy? Sagging with fatigue, he gave himself over to the soothing comfort of sleep.

He slept through the rest of the night. When he awoke, the faint light of morning was beginning to seep through the jungle. There were no signs of the night war but he dared not return to the camp in case of danger there. He stretched his cramped muscles, then left the niche, determined to walk to the village to face his father. It was all over. He wanted to go home.

He heard footsteps on the trail.

In the blink of an eye, he was back in hiding. Two figures appeared on the trail in the wan light. Hartmann Schele and Guy Garcia.

Hugh almost called out to them in relief before realizing that they could be the thieves. Maybe they'd waited out the gun battle, too, and were now coming to finish the theft.

But the two strode past the building, moving up the trail, passing within a few yards of Hugh, who made himself as still as possible.

He breathed a sigh of relief when they were gone, but now he was puzzled. The two men were supposed to be in the village along with the other evacuees, yet they didn't seem interested in the antiquities either, so what were they up to? The trail led to the wellsite and the cavern. Of course—he decided—they were heading for the cavern of gold! The antiquities in the storehouse could wait for another time.

He slid out of the niche and followed them from a safe distance.

Where the jungle trail opened into the grassy field, he stopped. Schele and Garcia stood near the *midden.* A moment later, a small troop of soldiers led by Lieutenant Ruiz joined them.

Hugh crept closer, camera in hand, determined to capture all of them on film. Crawling on his belly, he slithered behind a clump of low lying bush, as close as he dared go.

The men were relaxed, laughing. Ruiz lit a cigarette, blew the smoke into the cool morning air, then snapped his fingers at a soldier. He was brought a large duffel bag. Ruiz flicked aside the cigarette and opened it.

Money. Stacks of it. Ruiz was going to pay Schele and Garcia for the antiquities.

He froze as the cold metal of a gun barrel was jammed against his neck.

"Alt!" A soldier ordered.

The men in the clearing turned at the sound of the noise, staring at Hugh in surprise.

The soldier yelled at him again, prodding the gun into his back, forcing Hugh to get up. He shoved him toward Lieutenant Ruiz.

"Who are you?" Ruiz commanded.

Garcia stared at him in disbelief. "The boy! How…?"

Schele cut him off. "Well, well. Hugh Falkins. What an interesting surprise. We thought you had been evacuated."

Hugh clenched his fists in anger. "So it was you after all. We knew you were a crook."

"Did you?" he drawled with indifference.

"What are you doing here?" Garcia shouted. He stepped forward and slapped him across the face. "Talk!"

Hugh was rocked back on his heels. "We know everything," he said, trying to keep his voice steady. "You won't get away with this."

Schele's eyes narrowed quizzically. "I don't think he knows anything, Guy. I think he's alone. A lone hero."

"They do know," Hugh blurted out. "You won't be able to get them out of the country."

"What's he talking about?" Garcia asked.

"Nada. He knows nothing. But he does think we're common thieves. What is it you think we've stolen, Hugh?"

His voice was so calm, so pleasant, that Hugh was taken aback.

"Well?"

"The—the antiquities, of course. You stole them. Cut the carvings off the walls. Took the other things…"

"Antiquities?" Schele laughed generously. "Well, this is a surprise. My, my, my."

He was bewildered. Schele seemed to find the whole incident amusing. But the lieutenant was becoming impatient. He zipped the money bag shut and glared at Hugh. His hand went to the pistol at his waist.

"No," Schele ordered. "I'll take care of him. You'd better get going. I'll take that." He pulled the bag out of the lieutenant's hands.

The lieutenant grunted and turned away. He ordered his men toward the *midden.* And to Hugh's surprise, they pulled from a secret cache in the ground, only a few yards away from Linda's excavation, a bulky load covered with tarpaulins.

"Guns!" Hugh exclaimed.

Schele smiled coyly. "Assistance in a needy cause. Not the common thieves you thought we were. No, you see, Hugh, we've bigger fish to fry."

"Like starting a rebellion."

"Wrong again. Putting *down* a rebellion. As you likely know, we successfully repulsed a rebel crossing tonight…"

"Killed them, you mean."

"Scared them off, actually. A lot of noise but no real damage. However, their presence is a good excuse for the next phase of my plan. We'll hide these guns in some of the villagers' homes and when the lieutenant and his boys come knocking on their doors tomorrow looking for suspected rebels…"

"They'll be arrested. But they're innocent."

"The price of war. It's not my problem, is it?"

The soldiers shouldered the guns and filed out of the clearing. Shortly they were gone from sight.

"What about him?" Hugh pointed at Garcia.

Guy Garcia scowled at him. "I'm taking my cut as soon as the contract's signed and I'm outta here. Back to the U.S. of A."

"You're American? What contract?"

Schele consulted his watch. "Our real job. Contracted as advisors to the Mexican Federal Electricity Commission. I'm rather proud of the idea, myself. The F.E.C. wants this land as a flood basin for the power dam. But the people won't leave. So we simply show them proof that Yaxchilán is secret rebel stronghold, the army shoots off a few guns for effect, and then it forces out the locals for cooperating with the enemy. Mission accomplished. The way is clear for the F.E.C. to build a dam."

"But you'll flood everything," Hugh protested. "Homes, farms, the rainforest. And Yaxchilán too. It'll all be under water."

"All the more good reason for someone to remove the antiquities then, don't you think?" Schele thought this was tremendously funny and chuckled appreciatively at his own joke.

Garcia was anxious. "C'mon. We'll be missed. We've got to go."

"Of course," Hugh said. "I didn't see you at the evacuation. You were gone."

"Detained by the army," Schele said. "But Guy is right. Time to go. So," he paused dramatically, "what shall we do with you?"

Garcia pulled out a wicked looking blade. "Let me."

Hugh froze.

"No," Schele ordered Garcia. "I have a personal point to settle with this young man. First, tie his hands. I'll meet you later as planned."

Garcia was about to argue but thought better of it. In a moment, Hugh and Schele were alone. Schele pulled a pistol from his pocket. "Just in case you're thinking of running away. To the *cenote*!"

Hugh moved as well as he could with his hands tied but his own body, shaking with fear, betrayed his desire to escape. Schele was going to kill him. He had to run. But, instead, he found himself obeying.

They were at the edge of the pool in ten minutes, a nightmare walk that seemed to him like hours. The early morning light barely lit the cavern. The roar of the waterfall seemed unnaturally loud.

"What are you going to do with me?" he asked.

Schele smiled. "Patience, my young friend. We must wait for the dawn to rise above the *cenote's* lip. Then we'll begin."

"B-begin what?"

But Schele grabbed his ankles and tied them with grid cord. "I'll be back on time. I've been waiting for this, Hugh Falkins. I've been waiting for centuries."

He sagged. His will to move was gone. He could only watch the light as it slowly began to strengthen. He couldn't think straight.

When Schele returned, he was dressed in Mayan ceremonial garments. A white mantle covered his shoulders and a cap of blue feathers adorned his head. His wrists were ringed with gold and his arms, legs and face were painted blue. His hair was scooped up and tied into a topknot.

"Recognize me, Hugh? The *ahuacan*, the Mayan high priest."

"You're crazy."

"And now you." Schele slit the ropes and cords with a knife but he held a pistol to ensure Hugh made no sudden moves. "Strip," he commanded. "And put these on."

Hugh moved as if in a trance, his body obeying another set of laws. When he was finished, he wore only a white loincloth and bracelets of gold around his wrists and arms.

"I—I don't understand this. What's going on? Why are you doing this to me?"

"Your body will never be found. They'll just assume you've run away again. And no one will look for a psychologically disturbed young boy who's run off into the jungle." He smiled with self-satisfaction.

"Disturbed? What do you mean?"

"Oh, I know all about you, Hugh Falkins. I know more about you than you think. You hear voices, don't you? See strange things? Don't deny it, I know you do. Your father also suspects it because he behaves oddly too."

Hugh found the courage to speak. "I'll run, then. I won't tell anyone. They wouldn't believe me anyway."

"Oh, I know that. By the way, do you know what day it is?"

"What day?"

"It's the end of *Uayeb*, the end of the five unlucky days. It's also the end of the *tun*, the cycle of years. And do you know how the ancient Maya celebrated the end of the cycle?"

Hugh shivered with fear. What was Schele talking about? The man was crazy.

"They celebrated with a sacrifice."

A strange feeling flooded over Hugh. No longer fear but relief. He knew this moment was coming, he'd known it all along.

"One Shell! You're One Shell!"

"You know me, don't you? You know your destiny is to die on the altar of sacrifice. I have come back to make things right again. Lie down on the stones, Hugh."

He felt powerless against Schele. He could not disobey. The stones were cold against his back. He stared up into a brilliant sun just coming through the openings in the cavern. The jungle breathed softly. The animals were silent.

Schele began to pray in ancient Mayan while painting Hugh's body in blue designs.

He understood the man's words. He heard the prayers of priests. Smelled the heady incense in the air. Shadows played across his eyes.

He was ready.

An obsidian blade appeared in Schele's hand. He raised it above Hugh's chest, the blade glinting in the sunlight.

"Hugh! No!"

The shout shattered the spell. He jerked up as the blade descended, twisted under its speeding arc—but in doing so, lost his balance. Heard the blade clang against the stones.

And he was suddenly falling. Falling into the waters of the *cenote*.

CHAPTER 9

He screamed all the way down—down so far he imagined his lungs were going to burst. His ears roared with the sound of rushing water, with the sound of his own blood crashing against the walls in the cave of his mind. His head slammed against something hard and he almost passed out.

Just hold on—pool soon—should have been out by now—what?—taking too long—hurts—ohhhh—I'm a bird—flying—impossible—but—underwater bird—tunnel of light—great blue light—maybe—maybe I'm—DEAD!

He rose, slowly, forever it seemed, through a dark tunnel, bubbles rushing by him in a frenzy. A round, white opening beckoned. He broke the surface with a slight *pop*, gasping for air. Light poured down through his lungs; pure sunlight ran through his veins and the sky revolved around him in circles. "I'm spinning," he said to himself, and he sculled with his arms to slow the movement of his body and turn over on his back. He made it. But...where?

Above him, high towered rock reached up toward the blue medallion of sky. He was in a large pool open to the sky. People were leaning over the edge twenty feet above him, peering down, cheering, banging drums, whistling. He reeled with the light and noise.

Voices called to a sandy beach where hands reached out for him and pulled him in. He was naked except for a loincloth and gold bracelets around his wrists and ankles. He stood on wobbly legs while someone whipped a robe around him. The spinning in his head slowed.

"*Ah unic*," an old man said, falling to his knees, burying his face in the mud. The three men with him did the same. When he rose, they rose, they were smiling, chanting the words again and again. Then, the old man addressed him in an ancient Mayan language.

"We have been waiting for you, lord who returns to us from the underworld of *Xibalba*. We, poor creatures of Malenche, welcome you back and we are happy."

To his surprise and disbelief—he understood the words.

His arms and legs were painted blue, and when he wiped away the water droplets on his face, it, too, was blue. He brushed his hands over his hair that was pulled back and tied in a topknot. There was a ring on his finger in the emblem of a bird.

The people were shorter than he, their noses large, noticeably hooked, and their foreheads flat and sloping backward. His own was small and rounded. Their skins were also dark, his lighter.

Then who was he? Not one of them, obviously. He racked his mind for some knowledge but his head hurt too much. He vaguely remembered falling, hitting his head and someone calling "Who? Who?"

"My Lord returns from his ancestral home far away. I am your servant, Puuc, who is glad to have you back. Come, we will prepare your way."

"Yes. Of course," he sputtered hesitantly. "Lead on."

Glancing back, he saw a beautiful waterfall spurting out of a hole in the side of the walls, its cascading tumult falling to the green pond from which he had come. Further up, above the falls, the crowds were still cheering, their songs and drums reverberating in the air.

They proceeded up a steep trail which took them to the level above the pool, passing men and women who quickly threw themselves to the ground and buried their faces in the earth, averting their eyes from his.

"Why are they doing this?" He tugged at the old man's sleeve.

"Do they not honor you in your land?" The old man seemed only mildly surprised. "It is not proper to look upon you until the king welcomes you among his people."

"The king?"

"Bird Jaguar the Great. King of Malenche."

Puuc was the high priest of the temple of Yaat Balaam, founder of Malenche. His followers were priests of a lower order. Hugh understood it was their duty to care for him, to hide him away from human eyes until the proper ceremonies could be held to honor his return among them. He learned that he had been a prisoner of war, a foreigner, destined for sacrifice. High atop the *cenote*, the deep well, he had been prepared in the traditional way, stripped and painted and dressed for his entry into *Xibalba*. He should have died. The knife should have torn open his very heart and he should have been thrown to the waters below where he would sink from the weight of the gold he wore into the depths below.

But the knife had not penetrated his skin. He flew like a diving bird into the shining waters and rose back up to the surface, thereby defying the Lords of the Underworld. He must therefore have been sent to the people as a sign from the gods. His height confirmed it. His strange looks, his pale skin and long hair, the legends said, were the signs of one who would come back among them to save them.

"Save you?" he protested. "No. I'm, I'm..."

"Who?"

"Yes, Hugh." The name seemed right to him. He was Hugh. But Hugh who? If only his head would stop throbbing with pain, it would all make sense.

"Huu." The old man looked unperturbed. "You are called the Lord Huu, one of the Hero Twins who has come back from his long journey through the world below. We will call you Huu, as you wish."

It was all too confusing to him; he couldn't remember. His head hurt. For now he'd better play his assigned role until he could find out what had really happened to him.

"You shall help us win the war," Puuc said gently.

War? A shiver went up his spine. Had he been saved to fight a war?

Puuc seemed undisturbed. They would begin soon, he said. It was the time of *Uayeb*. They would attack the enemy when least expected and the Lord Huu would lead them to glorious victory.

The word of his—Huu's—arrival spread around the countryside like a storm that day. The *cahalob*, minor nobles and members of Bird Jaguar's court, and hundreds of his loyal subjects flocked to the plaza for the celebration, to see the tall white one who had escaped death. He was not allowed by the priests to see the preparations but was hidden away in a building high above the plaza. Yet he could hear the crowds far below as he lay back on the straw sleeping pallet and stared through a window into the night sky.

The jungle breathed around him. In the distance, drums pounded throughout the night. The plaza—he vaguely remembered being dragged as a blood-soaked, beaten prisoner along a gleaming white surface there—was some distance away and below him the mighty river, the Xocol Ha, swept toward the sea.

He had been fed well, bathed and perfumed and even now was dressed in a white knotted loincloth and a loose-fitting cotton shift. He smelled the heady tang of *pom*, a resin of the copal tree burned as an incense, floating on the air from the priests' fires. Their chanting went on all night in a dull, languid murmur. Only the nearby jungle was dark and strangely restful.

Who was he? He racked his thoughts for images of his past life but the days were a misty blur with strange pictures coming to him in snatches: flying in a white bird, a man puffing on a pipe, a golden earring. A knife raised above him...He tried to sleep, but his head continued to throb. From time to time he felt as if a great river were battering him. He heard the sound of a chattering beast, cries of men, and the spatter of loud fire. He understood none of it. There was a girl with red hair calling out to him from beyond the murky veil.

He must have slept. When he awoke, the sun had made its nightly journey through the underworld and was now reemerging to the sight of men. Its rays slanted through the doorway of the small room. He watched a lizard making its slow, patient way to a patch of that warm light.

Puuc burst into the room with a host of attendants. "I hope you slept well, Lord," he said, busily directing his priests. "The morning ceremonies will begin soon. We must be ready."

He was ushered into another bath, massaged until his body ached, then perfumed and powdered. He started to hum to himself a jingle—"You'll feel better with Oil of Olay"—but Puuc stared at him oddly so he stopped. His hair was cut and trimmed into a new topknot and adorned with a circlet of brilliant birds' feathers. He wore high-backed sandals, another clean loincloth and a pure white shift. Over it was fastened a cape of fiery swirling color. Finally, the jangling gold rings for his ears and nose.

"Ouch! Take it easy!" he squealed.

"You must be dressed well." Puuc forced the bangle through his ear. "Better than those lowly *cahalob*. I just can't wait to see the expression on that pig-dog, One Shell's, face when he sees you."

His eyes widened. One Shell?

But Puuc was grumbling as if dealing with an ungovernable child. "...and say nothing. Say nothing or as little as possible. Leave everything to Bird Jaguar."

"Why are you treating me this way?"

"It has been prophesied that you would come. There is so much to do. Stop squirming!"

He bit his lip petulantly. “I’m not a god, you know. I’m just…”

“Sst! Do as you’re told.”

He fumed. *Some way to treat a god*, he thought, *especially if I am one.*

The final touches to his costume were an emerald headdress and a staff of gleaming hardwood.

“Magnificent,” Puuc murmured appreciatively. The attendants nodded in agreement. “I hear the horn of announcement. Let us go, my Lord Huu, to meet your people and Bird Jaguar, the Great.”

Hundreds of people, resplendent in their finery, lined the plaza and riverbank. They were an army of colorful headdresses and gold ornaments sparkling in the early morning sun. The nobles, in the order of their importance, occupied the best positions along the steps of the largest white temple facing the plaza.

Priests and armed soldiers stood in wait near the doorway at the top of the temple itself. Inside, Hugh guessed, was Bird Jaguar, the ruler of Yaxchilán.

Yaxchilán. Malenche, Puuc called it, but he suddenly remembered it as Yaxchilán.

The brooding jungle was held back to reveal clusters of buildings arranged on the natural terraces of hills rising above the green river. The main group stretched out for a great distance along a gleaming plaza parallel to the riverbank; others were built in isolated positions on high ground above the plaza.

They stopped as a deep-throated, drawn-out trumpet echoed in the air. The crowd fell silent and went down as one to its knees, eyes averted.

His entourage approached in silence now, descending from a high terrace down a series of wide stone steps. There was something eerie about the slap-slap of their sandals in the unnatural silence. Under the heavy cape he was sweating badly and he wanted a drink of water but he was sure this would be frowned upon; the priests took their ceremonial duties seriously.

“The House of Hachakyum,” Puuc intoned.

A man accompanied by a boy appeared on the platform. They strode to a place in front of a small altar. Hugh’s breath caught in his throat. Even from far below, the taller figure was impressive for the way he carried himself with poise and strength.

Bird Jaguar.

Puuc took Hugh's staff from him and prodded him in the back. "From here, you go on alone. Your destiny awaits."

He trembled, unsure of himself, but there was nowhere else to go. He couldn't run. Not now. Taking a deep breath, he began the climb up the stairs. He felt the eyes of the nobles on him even though they were turned from his. They would be curious about this tall foreigner who had cheated death: some would doubt him, others would even be angry at his success. Halfway up the stairs, the strain on his legs made him stop. His breath came in short gasps. Vertigo nearly made him faint. He forced himself to go on.

When he made it at last to the platform in front of the king and the boy, they were alone, the priests and guards having withdrawn to the far end of the platform.

Bird Jaguar was impressive close up, taller than most of the other men, his face brooding, the mouth pursed in a thin, unwavering line. His large nose was hawklike, hooked in the way of the Mayans. He stood stiffly, legs planted firmly on the stone, muscled arms folded across his chest, narrow eyes riveted on Hugh. He was made even more inspiring by an iridescent headdress of quetzal bird feathers.

A smaller, younger Bird Jaguar, around twelve years old, glared at Hugh defiantly.

"Look at them," Bird Jaguar commanded in a deep voice. "Turn around."

He did so, dizzy with vertigo, but held himself steady. On the higher elevations surrounding him, thin wisps of mist still clung to the temples; on the plaza at his feet white stone glimmered in bright sunlight. Beyond it swept the green arm of the Xocol Ha River.

"They wait to see the stranger among us, the one who escaped the judgment of my knife at the well of sacrifice."

His eyes widened. "*Your* knife?"

"You don't remember? No, you were drugged to make you more willing to go to *Xibalba*. But," he grinned mischievously, "it appears it did not want you and spit you back."

Hugh was aware that he was being tested, that every word he said was important now. "I prefer the green paradise of Malenche and the hospitality of Bird Jaguar the Great."

"You were destined to help us, Lord."

The boy at Bird Jaguar's side spit contemptuously.

"My son, Chel-Te, who will be named Shield Jaguar after his grandfather, welcomes you also."

The king raised his arm. At once, the trumpet blared across the plaza and the people rose to their feet. The priests and guards repositioned themselves directly behind the three of them.

Bird Jaguar raised his voice and spoke to the assembled crowd, the concave bowl of the mountains and the stone walls carrying his voice clearly. He praised the gods for sending Lord Huu, their hero, among them, a sure sign of success in the impending battle. But first, there was to be a test.

Hugh gulped.

Puuc presented Bird Jaguar with a knife.

Puuc turned to Hugh who nervously focused on the obsidian blade. "Don't be afraid," he whispered, "it is a simple matter. Give me your arm. And don't cry out."

Puuc pulled stiffly on his arm. Another priest appeared with a bowl, which he thrust underneath the outstretched arm. Bird Jaguar didn't glance at him once. His gaze was reserved for the nobles lining the stairs. Hugh thought he read in those eyes seething disdain and anger.

The nobles stiffened with anticipation.

Puuc pulled back Hugh's clenched fingers and Bird Jaguar swept the knife once over his palm.

He didn't feel a thing at first. The incision was neat, shallow, and the blood flowed freely from the wound into the bowl. Only a moment later did the pain take effect, a hot jab of lightning across his palm, causing him to flinch. He bit his lip to keep from crying out.

Puuc then filled the bowl with pungent leaves and strips of bark. Over these, he sprinkled a heavy resin powder, which he set on fire. Heavy smoke poured from the basin into the air.

Bird Jaguar nodded to Puuc and the priest carried the bowl down the stairs being sure to let the nobles see the heavy smoke that rose from it. The whole affair was carried out in silence as if silence itself was the true test. Puuc returned with the bowl.

"It is good," he announced.

Bird Jaguar smiled.

From out of the temple doors two burly guards strode forward, dragging a man clothed in a loincloth. He was thrown on his back on the small altar and held there, facing up, his face stricken with terror.

Bird Jaguar moved to the other side of the altar and grabbed the man's topknot with his left hand. Hugh, mesmerized by the prisoner's fear, allowed Puuc to grab his right hand and place it around the topknot also. And before he could refuse, the king pressed his knife into Hugh's free hand and held on. The knife rose as if it had a will of its own. Their arms curved down in a wicked arc, plunging the knife into the man's chest.

The prisoner's scream ripped through the silence. Hugh let go, staggering back.

The king held the knife with two hands and ripped up with tremendous strength through the man's chest cavity while the two guards restrained the thrashing body. He carved and slashed and plunged his hands into the chest, yanking from it the man's gushing heart. Blood sprayed over his white tunic. "It is done!" he laughed. He shook the heart at the nobles, threw it in a long arc down the stairs like a bloody ball and, without a wasted motion, flung the corpse of the prisoner after it.

Hugh froze, bile rising in his throat. His own blood charged wildly through his body as the prisoner's continued to pour out on to the stone steps. He wavered, nearly fainting, but Puuc held him upright.

"Not now, Lord. Stand. Do not let them see that you are afraid."

He may have run if the crowd hadn't just then exploded in a fireworks of cheering, drumming and noisemaking. The king smirked at the nobles. Puuc's shoulders sagged and he breathed a sigh of relief.

Hugh was shocked and outraged, yet it was worth his life to say nothing. He had been accepted by the gods. He had passed the test. He could now be spoken to as an ordinary man. Puuc ensured that he was made known to the nobles of the court, so he learned quickly who was important and who was not. Those of most rank were related to Bird Jaguar himself and his mother's lineage.

Bird Jaguar's mother, Lady Eveningstar, had been a foreigner from a neighboring kingdom. So was his wife, Lady Great Skull Zero. And it quickly became apparent to Hugh that there were those who secretly hated the foreign element. The direct descendants of the late Lady Xoc, first and favorite wife of Shield Jaguar, Bird Jaguar's father, believed it should be one of her sons who should be king, not the upstart Bird Jaguar, son of his second wife.

The king, he decided, was having a tough battle without even going to war with another kingdom, which was why it was so important for him to have the approval of the gods in the morning's ceremony. Hugh was seen simply as living proof of Bird Jaguar's dominance over the other nobles and he wondered briefly if Bird Jaguar had even set up the whole affair just to reinforce his own power.

If he was just a pawn in a political game, what was his own status now? Some of the nobles still clearly distrusted him, Chel-Te hated him, and even the king seemed to think poorly of him. And what about Puuc? The priest could be more than the fawning attendant he appeared to be. Hugh guessed he would have to be very, very careful.

An armed warrior in the tunic of a noble stepped boldly in front of them.

Puuc blanched. "One—One Shell. I thought you were away at the war?"

The bronzed figure sneered. "You'd like that, wouldn't you, you sniveling snake. Trust you to plot when my back is turned. Now, let us see this man who cannot die." He turned to face Hugh directly.

Hugh stared back into the face of a man he knew. Tall, with a hawklike nose and cruel face, One Shell's other identity came back to Hugh in a flash. His temporary amnesia was swept aside like a curtain. And all at once, a dam burst in his mind, letting in a flood of forgotten images, images of a far-away world, of people and things that were more real to him than Malenche itself.

In that instant of recognition, he began to remember, not fully at first, but with increasing vividness. He wasn't Huu, the Mayan lord, he was Hugh. Hugh Falkins. He had fallen into a *cenote*, a tunnel into the past, into eighth century Yaxchilán. And somehow, it wasn't clear how, he knew that One Shell was a man named Schele.

He tried to keep his face expressionless.

And if Schele/One Shell recognized him, he was giving nothing away either. His eyes were stonelike. "From what kingdom do you come? You aren't Malenche."

"Kingdom, Lord?"

Puuc prodded him. "A little known place, Lord One Shell, far away near the sea."

"Tam-pah," Hugh blurted out.

"I don't know it."

"I've traveled far."

"Are all of you so ugly?"

"His people are all fair and they are tall like trees," Puuc suggested, trying to push Hugh out of the way.

"What king?" One Shell demanded.

Anger curled inside him. One Shell had no right to be belligerent to the Lord Huu and he wasn't going to back down. "Wash-in-tin," he replied, mustering up as much pride as he could in the name. "A king of great warriors." He must not lose face in front of One Shell.

One Shell sneered and moved aside to let them pass. Puuc propelled Hugh away quickly, his face showing signs of nervous strain. "Stay away from him, Lord. That one is the king's stepbrother and eldest son of Lady Xoc. He would like to claim the throne for himself." Puuc looked worried. "I know he is amassing an army of nobles to his cause."

Hugh nodded but he didn't give away his true knowledge of One Shell's identity.

"By the way, Lord Huu, I have never heard of Tam-pah. Is it very far?"

He smiled. "Yes, Puuc. Very far indeed." And then as an afterthought, he said, "I came on a great white bird."

Puuc cried in surprise.

Hugh rested after the morning's ordeal, the pain in his head having nearly gone. But he worried about what would happen to him. Would he ever get back to the twentieth century? Would his father be worried, too? Would the others care? What if Schele was right and they thought he'd just run away again? He'd have to try to make it back by himself. Mostly, though, he wondered what diabolical plot was being hatched by One Shell against him.

That afternoon they toured Malenche. The center was marvelous, more marvelous than the ruins of the twentieth century had ever suggested to him. The temples, which rose from the tree-shrouded forest, were so perfectly suited to the landscape that they seemed to flow with the contours of the steep-sided land. A high temple with a three-hundred-foot stairway leading up to it from the plaza dominated the site.

On the plaza itself, throngs of people milled about doing their daily business. As he passed among them with his company of guards, they now acknowledged him politely by pressing their palms to their foreheads. A man-made dock was clustered with scores of canoes that brought trade goods up and down the river. Business people spread their wares on the warm stones to display them to potential buyers. Mounds of fruit reminded him that he was hungry. Red, green and orange mountains of melons, squashes, yam, cassava, and corn delighted his eyes and his nose tingled from the spicy tang of red peppers. Women dressed in *huipiles* with red embroidery busily prepared *tortillas* whose scent wafted into the air.

He could stand it no longer and demanded to be fed. The *tortillas* were delicious and a feeling of well being came over him.

He strode by stacks of trade wares. There were colorful mantles with intricate designs, shawls, tapestries, sashes and resplendent bird feathers that sparkled like diamonds. He laughed at the sight of live fish splashing in clay-sealed baskets.

Someone was making a pot from river clay, squatting on the ground and turning it in his hands. It was being formed into the snout of a jaguar with ears curled back to form handles. Two rows of incised lines were the potter's trademark. Hugh admired it.

He liked the people, too. He was relaxed, happy. Until he heard the sound of the jaguar.

Pushing through the crowd toward the sound, he found the cat trapped in a cage barely large enough for it to stand in upright. Its owner beat the sides of the cage with a stick, causing the jaguar to snarl with rage. It twisted and pushed in the narrow confines of the reed bars but was helpless to move further. The man poked the stick inside to prove to a buyer the ferocity of his animal. The jaguar cried out in frustration, its yowl ripping through the air like torn fabric.

He boiled with rage. "Stop him!" he commanded Puuc.

The priest was indifferent. "It must not lose its ferocity, Lord. It is needed to scare our enemies. Once trained, the army will buy it for use in war or perhaps a noble will buy it to protect his property."

The seller caught sight of Hugh and his followers. "Lord, see this one. Truly, he is the fiercest animal I have ever seen." His eyes glinted with the prospects of a sale. "See how he cowers also under my common hand. You, a master, could train him easily." He poked the stick through the bars once more. The jaguar cringed and pulled back as far as it could go.

But Hugh was furious. He snatched the stick out of the man's hands. "I'll teach you about training," he cried out and lashed at the owner with the stick. He lashed again and again, forcing the man back against the cage. A paw flashed out.

The seller yelled in pain and fell to the ground. Puuc yanked the stick out of Hugh's hands. The crowd milled around to see the action, pushing and shoving against Hugh but he didn't care. He was still in a rage, his eyes glazed with the red of battle.

Then something struck him. Pain shot through his side. He put his hands to his thigh and found it drenched in blood. He suddenly felt weak and he stumbled against Puuc.

The priest's eyes widened in fear. He yelled at his guards and they swarmed around Hugh, pulling him away through the crowd. "Buy the cat," Puuc cried to one of his men. "You others. Take the lord away from here."

He was hurried to a place of safety.

"What happened?" he croaked. The blood was still seeping from a jagged wound in his thigh. "The cat?"

Puuc's eyes hardened. "It was no cat that struck you, Lord. Someone tried to kill you."

CHAPTER 10

He lay on a cot in his small room, listening. The sounds of the jungle at night which had started to become comfortable were now terrifying. Every screech, howl and croak sent a shiver up his back. Even the scuttling of mice across the stone floor made him twinge with suspicion.

Puuc had placed guards nearby for his safety.

A jaguar sent out a cry from somewhere within the compound walls, the one that Puuc had bought in the bazaar. He felt its pain as if he, too, haunted the narrow confines of a stone cage.

Someone approached the door. He rose quickly from the cot, ready to fight.

Bird Jaguar pushed aside the thin cotton drape over the doorway and entered. He wore a simple cloak against the cool of the night. His finery was gone. His shadow, thrown by the light from the torch in a wall sconce, flickered uneasily.

"Sit. We will talk."

Hugh did as commanded.

Bird Jaguar remained standing. "The *Uayeb* is upon us. Do you know it?"

"The five unlucky days."

"Of course, but a god would know this, though you are a strange god, if indeed, you are one."

"The *h'menob* have proclaimed me so."

"Those so-called nobles are a lot of scoundrels and cheats. What they proclaim is for their own good." Bird Jaguar paced back and forth in the small room. "With the *Uayeb* coming, who can I trust?"

"Why do you come to me?"

The king's face softened. "I need you. You are *ah-nunob*, by which we mean 'he who speaks our language brokenly.' It has been prophesied that such a one as you would come and you can help me."

"But how?"

"Hear me. The nobles don't care who is king here as long as their power is not thwarted. Puuc thinks he can control me. The nobles, those related to my father's first wife, Lady Xoc, have tried several times to kill me. And now that you have arrived to help me, their power is in danger of faltering in the eyes of the people. I need you, Huu, stranger from afar, gods' messenger, to prove I am the legitimate king of Malenche."

Hugh jumped to his feet. "That's why you staged the ceremony this afternoon. I see it now."

"We made the sacrifice together and the gods approved. The people are happy too. They believe you will assist us in the war against the Totil."

"But I'm no warrior."

"You will be."

He tried to protest but the king took him by the shoulder, silencing him. Bird Jaguar glared fiercely into his eyes. "You are a sign. And I say you will help me to win. Behold—"

A woman slipped into the room, a tall thin woman with fair hair, almost gold. She ignored him. She wore a simple white mantle and a jade necklace. Lowering herself to her knees, she sat back on her heels, placing her hands in her lap, and waited for Bird Jaguar to speak.

"Your mother. Lady Te-Xoc."

Hugh stared at the woman, dumbfounded. Her rounded nose and forehead, her smooth skin and fine features were unlike those of Bird Jaguar's people.

Bird Jaguar smiled. He took the Lady Te-Xoc's chin in his hand and raised her head. In the firelight, Hugh could see that she was crying, frightened.

"But—but she's not my mother!"

"What matters is what I say she is, though it is also true that she is a daughter of a far-off line of the family of Lady Xoc and of the great Six-Tun Bird Jaguar, my grandfather."

He couldn't take his eyes off the woman. "I think I'm beginning to understand. She's your wife then, related to the nobles who hate you but she also looks different enough to be—my mother. Do they know her?"

Bird Jaguar laughed aloud. "You're quick. Puuc said you would be. No, they don't know her—yet. I'll make her presence known and soon. It will protect me while we are at war."

The woman said nothing.

Hugh looked doubtful.

The king smirked. "Don't forget she may also protect you, too, Lord Huu."

But he was thinking of the attack on him that afternoon. Bird Jaguar's complex political plan might not be enough to save either of them.

"It is done!" Bird Jaguar said with finality.

Lady Te-Xoc rose. Hugh reached out to take her hand but the king pulled her away and sent her out the door.

"Tomorrow is the bloodletting ceremony, the final proof of your lineage. Puuc will tell you what to do. In the meantime, Lord Huu, stay here. You are not safe yet."

The morning air was cold. Mist shrouded the hills and even the plaza was hidden in a veil of white. Hugh stood before the entrance to the temple of Lady Xoc just off the plaza. Bird Jaguar had assembled a handful of nobles, the ones he thought most important, One Shell among them. The warrior stood imperious, oblivious to the cold, his eyes fierce and challenging, looking upon Hugh as something distasteful. Two priests and Puuc waited in attendance. A sad and miserable looking Chel-Te was there too.

Bird Jaguar's wives, Lady Eveningstar of Calakmul and Lady Te-Xoc, adorned in brilliant white *huipiles* and flowered headdresses, were at his side. Te-Xoc's eyes were glazed over; her footsteps faltered. Drugged, he guessed.

Bird Jaguar, careful to stage every move, waited until the moment Ancestral Sun climbed out of the well of the eastern horizon from the depths of *Xibalba* and rose into the sky.

Puuc gestured to Bird Jaguar and they moved forward into the temple. On the walls and on the doorway lintels were intricate carvings. Carved on the left lintel, Shield Jaguar, dressed in elaborate headgear, was holding a torch while his wife knelt before him.

Prayers were said. The smell of incense filled the air. Lady Te-Xoc almost stumbled but she was caught by Bird Jaguar and forced to her knees in front of him. Holding a shallow bowl within the circle of her folded arms, she readied herself with a calm that made Hugh anxious. The bowl was filled with strips of beaten bark paper, a rope the thickness of her first finger and a huge stingray spine. She closed her eyes in a deep trance and extended her tongue as far out of her mouth as she could.

Bird Jaguar took the spine wordlessly and without warning drove it through the center of her tongue.

Hugh recoiled. Bile rose in his throat and he gagged but the woman didn't flinch. Not a sound passed her lips as she took the rope and threaded it through the wound.

The blood fell from her lips, saturating the paper in the bowl at her chest, and dribbled down her chin in a red stream and over the white garment.

The king removed the paper and dropped it in a knee-high censer where Puuc set it on fire. Plumes of smoke rose into the air. Now Lady Te-Xoc pulled the last of the rope through her tongue. Her husband removed the flowered head covering and replaced it with a skull mask. She swayed and began to moan.

Puuc spoke in a hushed voice. "Seven Death, God of War, brother to the Sun, is among us. It is a signal. Look."

Black smoke billowed from the censer. Hugh dropped his jaw in amazement as it formed a great writhing column and from it the Double-Headed Serpent snaked upward. The shedding of Lady Te-Xoc's blood had materialized the god of war.

The king and nobles drew their own blood too, offering it to the god who was among them. Puuc, as he did the day before, slashed Hugh's palm with the spine but he was ready this time, only wincing at the brief pain. Puuc dropped the blood in the censer.

Another column of smoke rose, heavier than the first. Hugh's head began to spin. There was something in the smoke that made his eyes water. One Shell was mumbling in supplication, his belligerent attitude of the day before gone as he gazed upon the column.

The smoke curled and twisted in the air and began to twine around Hugh's shoulders. As it did so, it took a new shape, an animal shape—the appearance of a double-headed jaguar.

He was afraid at first but, as the smoke jaguar enveloped him, he sensed a newfound power surging within him, a wave of radiant energy. He glowed with it.

He *was* the jaguar.

The king was shocked—his face pale, his voice ragged. But he was quick to grasp the opportunity. "Behold," he said, "the gods send us a sign to prove the power of the warrior who will lead us to victory in war, the power of the son of the Lady Te-Xoc, herself of the lineage of the great Lady Xoc."

He looked at Hugh. "Behold my son—Blood Jaguar."

* * *

Later, when the smoke had cleared and the nobles gone, Hugh and Puuc were alone. Puuc snorted with pleasure. "Heh, heh. What a sight. They nearly wet their loincloths. The nobles were struck by fear. Fear of you, Lord Huu—or should I say, Lord Blood Jaguar. They are now running through the countryside like monkeys with their tails between their legs, spreading the word of your transformation. There will be trouble from them no longer."

Hugh's eyes watered. He filled his lungs with fresh air. A sense of normalcy was beginning to return to him. "Where's my mother?" he asked.

"The ladies have retired. Their task is done."

"I want to talk to her."

"It is not possible. Bird Jaguar forbids it."

"My own mother? I demand it!"

Puuc was stubborn. "The woman is gone."

"Gone where?"

"It is of no consequence." Puuc waved his hand dismissively. "Come. There are things we must do."

Hugh grumbled but he knew that he would be wiser to heed Puuc's—or Bird Jaguar's—orders. In good time, he told himself, maybe he'd be giving the orders. He didn't like being tossed around like a ball at their command.

For the next two days though, he was too busy to think of the whereabouts of his appointed mother or to question the strange events that had taken place. They were preparing for war.

Malenche swarmed with people. The river bustled with canoes bringing goods from afar and the plaza was an anthill of activity. Every hour priests blessed warriors with acrid incense fires and the scent of sweat; dust and copal hung in the air. Vendors yelled out the cost of their wares. Soldiers paraded through the plaza to the beat of drums and the rattle of shells. Commands issued by brightly clad leaders were like the squawks of parrots and macaws. The screams of animals rent the air.

It was no different in the nearby villages. Malenche itself was only the religious center of a much wider state containing numerous small villages. Just above it was the largest village with its own well fed by the underground river, the source of the waterfall that exploded out into the *cenote*. The memory of falling through its roaring tunnel filled him with both dread and longing.

In the village, pigs and chickens were slaughtered as food for the army, then loaded onto the backs of slaves for transport to the war canoes. Clubs and knives, spears and bows were manufactured, as were stone-studded cotton armor, helmets, padded gloves and shields.

He visited the villages as the gods' emissary to encourage the preparations for war, but he was disturbed at the thought of what was to come.

The priest only scoffed at him. "It is an honor to go to war. All our young men crave it."

"But hundreds will die."

"They will receive glory or they will die. Of course."

His dismay was not relieved even when he discovered that the war with the Totil was a formally arranged affair. There were rules to be followed and prisoners would be exchanged at the end. But many would die, nevertheless, and the nobles and kings who were captured could expect to be sacrificed. The price of capture was the loss of the kingdom itself.

He was shocked. The idea seemed more brutal than the outright killing. "But Bird Jaguar could lose everything."

"Yes." Puuc was unconcerned. "The gods will determine who has the right to win and the right to be king. It is so."

"It's barbaric."

Puuc seemed puzzled. "Do you not war with other tribes in Tam-pah? How do your young men receive honor and glory?"

"Basketball," he said.

"What is that?"

"It's—it's a game."

"A game," Puuc sniffed. "Are the losers sacrificed to the gods?"

He shook his head in protest. "No, of course not. They lose the game."

"Very strange," Puuc decided. "It is honorable to die but not to lose."

Someone was in the room. Hugh woke from an exhausted sleep, a deep dark well from which he emerged in terror. He opened his eyes to near darkness.

The small fire in the brazier was a dull glow. A mosquito droned near his ear but he dared not slap at it. He waited to hear movement.

Turning his head toward the doorway, he saw only the faint outline of its rectangle. The cotton drape covering it barely moved. Far off, thunder coughed. Lightning flashed.

In its light, a man came for him, lunging through the doorway, a wicked blade gleaming in his hand. It swiped the air inches from Hugh's chest.

He rolled off the cot, lashing out with his foot and struck his assailant.

"Oof!" the intruder grunted.

Now he could make out the bulk of the man against the faintly illuminated doorway and he moved away.

The attacker rose and came at him again. Hugh feinted to his left and rolled to the right as the blade swished through the air a second time.

They circled each other warily, breathing hard. Hugh saw the extinguished torch in the sconce and yanked it out, plunging it into the brazier. The pitched reeds caught immediately, making a small explosion, and the room flashed into brightness.

Momentarily blinded, the attacker backed away, trying to adjust his eyes to the light. He whipped off a dark mantle he'd been wearing to free his movements and he approached with the knife held steadily in his hands, his mouth etched in a snarl, eyes glinting like obsidian stones in the torchlight. He lunged.

Hugh instinctively jabbed the fiery brand toward him and the man reared back in surprise, dropping the knife. He swept the torch again, driving him against the wall.

Hugh was searching for the knife when he saw Chel-Te huddled in the corner. "What? What are you—?"

In that instant, the intruder swept past him and grabbed the boy. He spun the king's son in his thickset arms and yanked the boy's knife from its belt.

Chel-Te squealed with fear.

"Put the knife down or I'll kill the boy."

Hugh gulped. But he calmed himself. "Who are you? Who sent you?"

The man let out a short, ragged laugh. "One who knows Bird Jaguar's conniving tricks. You're no messenger from the gods. You can't fool me."

He shifted closer. "Who told you to do this?"

"What are you talking about? Move back. The boy will die anyway."

He took a deep breath. Couldn't make a mistake now. The man would kill the boy.

"Are you sure your master will reward you well? When he hears you've failed, he won't be happy. And when he hears you've killed the boy instead of me, he'll turn that knife on you."

Chel-Te had been waiting for his chance. He lurched out of the man's grip and slammed his foot down hard into the intruder's instep.

The attacker howled and released his victim, who darted out of the prison of his arms. Angered, the attacker charged.

Stopped. In surprise. For a moment his eyes pleaded with Hugh to explain his sudden, incomprehensible pain. A huge spear quivered upright in his chest before his blood gushed out in spurts and he staggered against the wall. Then he slid to the floor with a dazed expression on his face and slumped over.

"Father!"

Chel-Te ran to the arms of Bird Jaguar who hugged his son to his chest. The king spoke to the boy quietly before he turned to Hugh. "I hope the gods grant you more lives. You seem to need them."

Hugh released the tension in his body. "I'll make a special prayer to the god who sends kings as protectors of their guests."

"Fathers and sons. Blood Jaguar lives."

"I think I know who sent him if you'd care to hear."

"One Shell. I know already," the king replied. "But I must guard you more carefully."

"How did you know I was in danger?"

Bird Jaguar sent his son away and commanded a pair of guards to remove the slain attacker. When they were gone, he asked Hugh to join him on the stone bench outside the room. The guards, off at a discrete distance, could not hear them.

Above, the stars began to go out, blotted by incoming rain clouds. The air was charged with the promise of lightning, and a few moments later they saw it splinter the sky with a resounding crack and heard thunder rumble across the sky. Hugh flinched, remembering the image of the guerrilla attack. But the storm was still some distance away. They sat in silence a long while before Bird Jaguar spoke.

"The thunder is a sign. The sign of war. Do you fear death, Blood Jaguar?"

"I—I—yes. I think I do."

"Then you are not wise. Death is nothing. Living is everything."

"Then why go to war? Surely, you may die tomorrow."

"I will die someday. If I die, I hope to die in an honorable war. I want the gods to carry me safely to *Xibalba*, there to join my father, Shield Jaguar, where we will live many more lives. But I fear, too."

"Who? Your enemies, like the one sent to kill me?"

"No. I fear for my son, Chel-Te. My father lived his life trying to make the way for my succession. I must do the same for my son."

"You're a good father to Chel-Te. I see it in the way you hold him and love him."

"Did not your father, also?"

"Are you not my father, too?"

"For the while I will act as one to you."

Hugh watched the stars blotting out one by one. In the other world he had two fathers, which was like having no father at all. But if he had to have a father in this world, he would wish for none better than Bird Jaguar. It would be good. But he also knew it couldn't last.

"I will do all I can to make Chel-Te's life safe and prosperous," Bird Jaguar stated softly. He stood up.

Lightning cracked again, a jagged scar across the face of the night.

"Do you know why Chel-Te was in your room tonight?"

"No."

"He wanted to kill you."

Puuc's face whitened. "My Lord, we have failed you. You must be protected at all costs." The priest looked frail, tired, not his usual self.

Hugh privately began to wonder if the preparations for war and the political strategies were just too much for the old man. He looked exhausted.

"I'm sure the young Chel-Te will be well chastised by his father for such foolishness. We have enough to worry about without the pranks of a young boy. And you must watch your back for those who are jealous of your kinship with the king."

"Like the *h'menob*, perhaps?" someone said.

They turned as One Shell broke in on their conversation. The powerful noble looked resplendent but dangerous in his thick armor and skull headdress of war. He was surrounded by four warriors.

Puuc was servile. "Why, whatever do you mean by that Lord One Shell? Surely the nobles are the vigilant protectors of the throne?"

The warrior ignored the priest and spoke to Hugh. "We are honored by your presence, *my* Lord Blood Jaguar. The name is a strong one, for I saw with my own eyes your transformation to the most fierce demon of the jungle."

Hugh chuckled inwardly. Two could play that game. "One Shell, *my* Lord. I have heard of your many exploits from others. I will be yet stronger to know I am guarded by the noblest of the *cahalob*, the strongest of the warriors."

"I serve Malenche."

One Shell's friends murmured approving sounds.

"Naturally. It does you honor to remember our father, Shield Jaguar, who made Malenche great. We should all serve our fathers who are our masters."

A shadow flickered over One Shell's face. "I am curious. You are not from the land of the green stones. You are *ah-nunob*."

"One who speaks the language brokenly."

"But your features are not ours. Your mother did not press your skull between boards to flatten your forehead as a sign of nobility. Your nose is small. And ugly."

Hugh did not rise to the bait.

"You are pale and your eyes are wide apart. You are not one of us."

"Not noble at all—" one of the others began but One Shell cut him short.

"I saw the jaguar in the smoke. He is a god. I think he is a god. If you do not die in battle, then you are a god."

Hugh stared into the eyes of the bronzed warrior. "I will not die, Lord One Shell. You will see to it that my back is well guarded at all times in case I have cause to worry."

"I will be behind you. Be sure of that."

The rain began to come down again. One Shell strode away quickly with his four guards, One Shell who wanted him dead. Hugh suddenly felt very cold and vulnerable.

There were two more political moves that Bird Jaguar made before they headed for war. Hugh was to have a stone tree dedicated to him, a pillar of stone carved with his likeness and telling the story of his arrival and reincarnation as Blood Jaguar. It was half-complete. After the victories in the coming war, Blood Jaguar's further exploits would be kept forever in stone for all to see.

The other was the beginning of his own temple.

Chac, the rain god, was not, however, proving helpful to Bird Jaguar's plans. The rain sheeted down heavily. Walking on the slick trails was difficult. The king was dejected. Only a few of the nobles had come to watch as the stone pillar was being dragged down the trail from a nearby rock quarry toward its destined resting place, the foundations of the new temple. The going became worse. Rain pounded the forest, turning the ground into a quagmire. The massive stone tower, pulled by slaves, rolled along hundreds of logs at a slow, grinding pace.

Hugh stared at the stone tree. He saw the unmistakable profile of a jaguar's head, a fierce, snarling face, warlike, carved to demonstrate menace and power.

Him. Blood Jaguar.

But he was feeling sullen and cold and miserable and desperately alone, not at all powerful. His plumed headdress and mantle were soaking wet. He trod in mud up to the tops of his sandals. And he was watching his back.

No one heard the rope snap in the drowning torrent of rain. One moment the stone tree was poised at the lip of an embankment, the next it suddenly swung in an unexpected arc and slammed into the slaves pulling it. Several went over the edge, screaming. He watched helplessly as the stone monster took on a life of its own. The jaguar screeched and plummeted down the hill, crushing a dozen puny men in its way, throwing up logs and mud like toys. It ploughed a deep furrow in the earth and at the bottom of the incline came to an abrupt halt.

Hugh gaped, his eyes wide.

The pillar rose as if it had decided to walk by itself, perfectly vertical. And then it swung through the arc, falling in a dangerous curve, smashing those below. It slammed into the earth and cracked.

The face of the jaguar snarled once more and disappeared beneath the mud.

CHAPTER 11

The sky ripped open. A storm slashed Malenche with malicious fury—a jaguar god throwing lightning bolts, ripping at the jungle foliage, bowing trees until they bent over like sacrificial victims at the altar. If the skies had poured blood, Hugh would not have been surprised.

War preparations came to a standstill. Soldiers cowered in the lee of the hills, the priests in the deep recesses of their temples and the nobles were nowhere to be seen. Only Bird Jaguar and Hugh, it seemed, were alive in Malenche. The king stood at the doorway of his great hall with a dark scowl on his face. He had been deeply moved by the toppling of the stone tree, yet none of his commands or shouts or insults would move the slaves or nobles to have it righted. They believed it was a bad omen.

Hugh knew better than to disturb the king. Returning to his own room, he slept, and in his dreams he saw the archaeological camp again, sheets flying in the wind, tents flapping like great orange birds trying to break free of the ropes that tethered them to the ground. The archaeologists tried desperately to secure their shelters. A great tree came crashing down.

When he awoke, he stretched his cramped muscles and wrapped a mantle about him to keep out the cold. The brazier beat a red heart but did little to warm the room.

The faces of the archaeologists and that of his father paraded before him like ghosts. Holding his head in his hands, he sobbed with loneliness and despair. He was in a pocket of time from which there was no escape.

The storm ended as abruptly as it had begun. And Bird Jaguar whipped his army back into order. The reappearance of the sun did more than his fury, however, to have the soldiers working with feverish activity and singing, too.

The ominous signs of the *Uayeb* were soon forgotten. This would be a glorious war.

They went by river; traveling fast, for the Xocol Ha was in full spate, gorged by the rainwater. They sped through the canyons, hundreds of canoes brightly colored with fantastic designs, their riders chanting loudly in unison, the sound echoing off the canyon walls and scaring up flocks of egrets in the trees.

Hugh's blood coursed strongly and he tingled with excitement when only a short while ago he had been tired and dispirited. The sun shone warmly on his arms. Where he sat with Bird Jaguar, in the most lavish of the canoes painted as his namesake—a great leaping jaguar with the quetzal headdress of a warrior—he felt proud to be leading the army of shouting men.

The Totil had been squabbling over territorial rights with Malenche for years and Bird Jaguar was out to teach the aggressors a lesson. It aggravated matters that the Totil had recently made an alliance with Bird Jaguar's traditional enemy from Palenque.

They reached the battleground and as they lined themselves on the floodplain, the Totil were waiting. At the head of their ranks was the *nacom*, the Totil general, Jeweled Skull, arranged in a magnificent feather headdress, which made him look taller than the others. His jewelry flashed in the sun.

But neither side seemed to be in a hurry. Bird Jaguar arrayed his men in a semicircle with the first class of warriors, the Order of the Jaguar. On the outside were secondary ranks. Inside the arc was a second line of defense, of peasants who had been pressed into service, and behind their protected lines, slaves and women who traditionally accompanied the army.

Food was the first order of the day. "An army does not fight without a full belly," Puuc said sagely. As they ate, he said, "The prime purpose of war is not to kill but to capture prisoners, particularly the *nacom*. Once he is taken, the battle is over and he will be taken away to be sacrificed."

Hugh choked on his corn, spitting it out in surprise. He just realized that *he* was the *nacom* of Malenche.

"These formalities, however, do not mean that many will not die."

Hugh saw that the lower ranks that had less protective gear would be vulnerable. The fields would be bloody that day.

Bird Jaguar looked invincible in his quilted cotton armor soaked in salt brine to harden it. His shield was enormous. The jaguar pelt, which covered his body, quivered with life. Hugh stole a glance at the Totil king in the distance. No less regal, Ruby Snake's body rippled with the sinuousness of a reptile.

* * *

A conch shell trumpeted the charge. The air exploded with warriors yelling and screaming, drums beating, pipes screeching. The armies, like two massive animals, plunged into one another.

A stone whistled by Hugh's head and he ducked unceremoniously as it slammed heavily into the skull of the man next to him. He jumped into the midst of a ferocious melee, swinging madly with his club, and was rewarded with the crunch of bone. He lunged, batted, jabbed. The din was ferocious.

Briefly, he saw One Shell cut down a man.

Then someone caromed into Hugh, sending him sprawling, and he looked up to see a club descending toward him. But, suddenly, it was knocked away and Bird Jaguar felled his would be assailant with a sword. "You cannot die," he shouted above the storm. "We must win."

Hugh returned the favor a moment later, knocking away a dagger arcing toward the king's back. The battle raged on until the Totil conch blared again, stopping it as quickly as it had begun. The armies fell back, leaving a wide gap between them, glad for the respite.

"I thought war was supposed to be honorable," Hugh gasped, trying to control his breath. "These guys are actually trying to kill me." His heart was pounding and he knew that real terror was just on the other side of the will to survive.

Bird Jaguar's face contorted in disgust. "The Totil are not honorable. They do not take prisoners for sacrifice to the gods. I dreamed that many would die."

"What do we do now?"

"What else? Fight. I mean to have Ruby Snake's head at my feet."

He strode to the head of his men, facing Ruby Snake and the Totil, shouting insults at them, despising their mothers, calling them dogs and vultures for invading the territory of Malenche. He expounded on the virtues of their most famous warrior, Blood Jaguar, sent from the Underworld to do war with them.

The Totil king stepped forward to return the insults and he called forward his *nacom*. There was a hushed silence as the burly figure strode into the open.

"Jeweled Skull!"

The armies whispered the name together, sending a shudder through Hugh. The man was tall and well muscled. He wore a simple loincloth, gold anklets and bracelets, but unlike the other warriors, he scorned any armor. His weapons were the lance and club and a wicked-looking dagger that protruded from a belt. With a flourish, Jeweled Skull donned the headpiece from which he got his name, a great bear's skull studded with flashing jewels, flourished with quetzal feathers.

Bird Jaguar spat disdainfully. "The Totil have no *nacom* of their own worthy of the name," he shouted at Ruby Snake. "They have to pay an ugly thug from Palenque to do their work." He looked at Hugh. "Here, take this," he said, handing him a wicked-looking trident made with razor sharp shells and tipped with the stingray's spines.

"Why?"

"He is yours. Do not fail."

Hugh wanted to run.

The battle catapulted into action again, and in a moment, he was fighting for his life again. He lost sight of Bird Jaguar but saw One Shell lift an enemy warrior off his feet with a powerful sweep of his club. He caught Hugh's gaze and shook the club at him.

A warning from One Shell was not to be ignored but he was becoming tired. He'd have to reach Jeweled Skull now before he was unable to go on.

The Totil warrior turned, sensing Hugh behind him, lashing out quickly.

The spear sliced across Hugh's chest protector. Jumping aside, he plunged with the trident, striking his enemy's shield a glancing blow, but Jeweled Skull was light and quick on his feet. The Totil warrior suddenly rolled, kicking Hugh's feet out from underneath him. The warrior smiled and pulled his knife.

Hugh rolled, using the trident to spring back to his feet before the knife could be used.

Jeweled Skull nodded his approval.

Hugh circled warily, oblivious of the battle around him. He knew Bird Jaguar could not protect him now. Swiftly dropping to the ground, he scooped up a handful of mud and threw it at the jeweled head. It took the man by surprise, his mouth open, and Hugh struck with the trident. It glanced off the warrior's ribs but made no effect. Jeweled Skull lashed out, forcing him back.

Then Hugh was hit from behind and suddenly he was down on his knees.

At the last moment, he looked up to see a great club swinging in an arc at his head. Lightning crashed in front of his eyes. His head snapped back and he fell to the ground, unconscious.

Hugh awoke with a crushing headache. His neck felt as if it were broken and, when he tried to open his eyes, the jab of light hurt so much that he immediately closed them and fell into unconsciousness again.

When he finally did come to, it was night. He lay on his side on a cold stone slab, his arms twisted behind his back and tied.

He jerked himself awkwardly to a sitting position in the dark. He was in a small room where, through an opening ten or fifteen feet above him, he could see stars blinking. He last remembered Jeweled Skull's club swinging and then a tremendous pain—but where was he now? The night was quiet. Once or twice, he thought he heard the shuffle of feet above him and someone clearing his throat. Likely a guard, not that Hugh was going anywhere.

Where was Bird Jaguar? The armies? Puuc? He shifted his weight and unintentionally banged his head against a wall. A shower of sparks exploded before his eyes and a spear of pain jabbed *inside* his head. "I won't do that again," he mumbled. He imagined leaning his head against a soft shoulder and he smelled the faint perfume of…

"He is awake. I must speak with him," someone demanded.

"Only a moment or you'll join him."

Puuc came down the stairs bearing a torch. He smiled gravely. "Are you well, Lord?"

Hugh groaned.

Puuc produced a knife, slitting the bonds around Hugh's wrists to allow him to work the blood back into circulation.

"I've brought you something to eat."

"Am I a prisoner?"

"Yes."

"Whose?"

"Ruby Snake's, of course."

"And where are we?"

"Eat this." He produced several large fruits, which Hugh devored greedily. "Well, you haven't lost your appetite," the priest said. "That's good. You'll need it."

Hugh finished the fruit and licked his fingers loudly. "So, what happened to me? Why are you here?"

"So many questions. Listen, I have only a few moments. You are back in Malenche. The Totil have put you in Bird Jaguar's care for now. A most unusual occurrence has taken place."

"Yes. Blood Jaguar, your famous warrior, has failed you. They'll sacrifice me, I suppose."

"The Totil have captured our *nacom*, yes. But we also have theirs. It's a draw."

Hugh's jaw dropped. "Jeweled Skull? How?"

Puuc was deferential. "You defeated him in battle, Lord. He'll be sore tonight."

"He hit me. I lost consciousness."

"As you did him. There is no clear winner. So the contest will be decided in the courts."

"The courts?" Hugh was confused. "Am I on trial for something? Do I need a lawyer? I know nothing about your…"

"What strangeness you speak, Lord. I mean the ball courts."

"Basketball courts?"

Puuc pursed his lips impatiently. "I mean the ball courts, my Lord Blood Jaguar. You and Jeweled Skull. You must win the game so Bird Jaguar can defeat the Totil."

"What if I lose?"

But he already knew the answer.

A day passed in the confines of the small room. Bats skittered high above in the dark recesses of the room. The night before, he had seen them, *zotz*, evil creatures who hunted in blackness. They flooded out of the window at dusk and returned at dawn, gorged.

If he felt any solace in his captivity, it was that Jeweled Skull must be nearby, also suffering the same isolation, cold and worry, sitting in slimy waste dropped onto the floor by the bats.

Much later in the day he was taken from the room and brought to another, one with a straw pallet and a charcoal burner for warmth. He imagined that Puuc or Bird Jaguar might be responsible for the better treatment. But he was still guarded.

Sleep did not come any easier for all that. In his dreams he played basketball against an opposing team called Team Yax, made up of tall bearded archaeologists and golden-haired women dressed in white, tight-fitting clothes and straw hats. The men smoked pipes and laughed and the women shouted incomprehensible things at each other about glyphs and strata and the time periods. They pointed at him and waved their fingers in circles around their heads to indicate that he was crazy. And the crowd was worse, ghostly blank-faced figures, whose laughter echoed around a vaulted roof. Laughing, all of them, laughing and pointing and waving their fingers at him. He had no team. He was all alone.

Music. It came from beyond the doorway and over the wall, the haunting sound of someone singing to the accompaniment of a flute. It was low, filled with unimaginable grief, a dirge that tore at his emotions as he went to the door. He saw only the shadowy form of the guard; all else was in darkness. He yearned to walk out and go to it—it was for him, he knew—and to the singer who was as much a prisoner as himself. His mother.

The song changed, as if she suddenly understood that he was listening. It became softer, sweeter, comforting. He felt that she was reaching out to hold him, to prepare him for his death.

When the song ended, the familiar sounds of the jungle, stilled by the music, rushed in to regain the night.

The next morning reminded him of his first day in Malenche. Puuc yanked him from his bed and propelled him into the arms of his priests. For the next hour he was massaged unmercifully until his body felt beaten. "It is nothing compared to what you will feel later," Puuc snapped back at his complaints. "You must be made ready." Then he was subjected to a steaming sweat bath, perfumed and fed. Something in the food surged through his body like a fire. He had to admit he was beginning to feel like a new man— enormously confident, powerful, ready to take on the world.

The priest tried to explain the nature of the ball game to him but Hugh scarcely paid attention. "Relax, man. I'm a natural," he grinned. "Let's spot these guys ten. Make it interesting. Wait'll they see my slam dunk."

He rattled on like a drunken parrot while Puuc shook his head, mumbling, wearing a worried frown.

Puuc and several Totil guards led him across the plaza amidst waving and cheering. Music echoed off the walls. The sun shone on the white stones. They entered the ball court.

His adrenaline-pitched confidence fell.

The court was a flat stone surface thirty or more paces long, rectangular in shape with sloping walls and decorated with red and blue markers at either end. On the floor in the middle was a large painted oval. Forty feet above, where the walls levelled out, tiers of seats were filled by boisterous spectators, on one side the nobles from Malenche, on the other the Totil, each dressed in their finery. In the middle of each, occupying an elaborate throne, were Bird Jaguar and Ruby Snake.

A game was in progress. *Pok-a-tok*. Each of two teams of seven men in padded clothes fought to knock a solid rubber ball the size of a human head past the end zone markers. The ball could not be thrown with the hands nor kicked—it had to bounce off heavily padded hips, shoulders and forearms.

The nobles screamed with excitement. They gambled against each other for high stakes—jade, gold, houses and slaves—anything they owned. Only the kings sat impassively. Their stake, Hugh understood, was higher.

The teams were near exhaustion when a Malenche player sent the ball spinning in an arc past the line of Totil defenders. The crowd roared with wild fervor. The winning team was ecstatic, the losers fell to the ground, stunned. Those who bet on the losers tried to run away from paying their debts.

The crowd fell silent as the captain of the losing team appeared before Bird Jaguar. He removed his protective clothing, placing it in front of the king and bowed his head.

Bird Jaguar rose slowly, insolently. His eyes flashed across to Ruby Snake and he waited. Glaring back, the Totil king raised his thumb to his mouth and bit on it showing acceptance of defeat by Bird Jaguar's side.

A knife flashed in the sun. The captain screamed once and Bird Jaguar held the bloody decapitated head in his hands. He flung it to the nobles and kicked the headless body, still spurting red, down the steps past a wide-eyed Hugh.

"Come," Puuc commanded. "It's your turn."

Hugh, trembling, lowered his head.

Puuc glared. "Not that. I mean, it's your turn to play. Get dressed."

He was prepared by the priests. Cotton padding went around his pelvis and a thick cloth around his forearms. Kneepads and elbow pads were added and a calf-length skirt went over the loincloth. Finally, a u-shaped yoke went around his waist to protect him if he fell.

Puuc said, solemnly, sadly, "This equipment has been passed down from father to son for many years. First it was Six-Tun Jaguar's, then Shield Jaguar's. Now your father passes it to you. Wear it well."

Hugh was in a daze, the image of the dead captain in his mind.

The teams were waiting. Malenche exploded with excitement as he made his way with his team into the court. At the other end was Jeweled Skull, an enormous, formidable man. He held his hand to his bandaged ribs and yelled something Hugh couldn't hear in the noisy arena. But the message was clear.

Hugh mustered all the confidence he could find, raising his head high. He sneered at the other and pointed to his own back. Message: there's no one to hit me from behind now. It's you and me. He glanced up at Bird Jaguar. The king sat impassively as stone. On one side of him was One Shell, on the other, Chel-Te.

He guessed now, with a clarity that was frightening, that the ball game had been planned all along. He was merely the player who was expendable. And he also guessed who had hit him from behind.

The teams lined up across the court on either side of the oval. Not merely a decoration, it was a portal into the otherworld where the gods were watching the game.

An official rolled the ball across the court and the two teams charged. Hugh rammed into the ball the same time as Jeweled Skull. It was like hitting a stone wall. He hammered again and the ball went skittering off among the players. The action was fast and furious. He was battered by the opposing players whenever possible; there was nothing in the rules about not hitting the other team. A Totil player upended him, knocking him to the stone floor. He forced himself to his feet, thrusting aside players in an attempt to get the ball but his breathing was hard, his blood pounded in his veins. He drove an elbow into a face, satisfied to hear the crunch of teeth.

A Malenche player dropped with fatigue. The play was halted and the body rudely dragged off the court to be quickly replaced by another player.

Jeweled Skull managed to free the ball. He kicked illegally with his knee and it went off the wall at a crazy angle toward the boundary marker. Hugh sprang into the air, off balance, to field the ball on his yoke.

He saw his chance finally as the ball bounced between two players. Using his forearms, he batted the ball with all his might.

Jeweled Skull floated through the air, butting it down with his head.

Hugh lunged for the ball, missed. He rose to one knee and Jeweled Skull charged into him, knocking him back. He hit the stone floor with a resounding *whump*, cracking his head. Lights flashed. He felt groggy. Had to get up. Stumbled for the end marker.

One of his players stopped the Totil from scoring with a dramatic leap but the ball bounced backward into play. The Totil player nudged the ball over to Jeweled Skull. Calmly, boldly, the warrior captain approached the ball.

Hugh glanced around. There was no one between Jeweled Skull and the marker except himself but he was heavy with fatigue. The sky wavered before his eyes as he staggered forward and went down in a heap.

Jeweled Skull batted the ball with his knee. It rose like a small sun and flew in a long arc over Hugh's prone body. Hugh turned in despair and watched it sail past the marker.

"Your father, the king, wishes to see you now," Puuc said.

Hugh was back in the prison cell, despair like a heavy weight on his shoulders. He had failed; therefore Bird Jaguar had lost everything. He had failed his father.

"I said your father is here," Puuc repeated snappishly. "Please don't let him see you like this." The man looked old, exhausted, and angry.

Hugh had come to like the priest in spite of his overbearing nature, and now Hugh realized he had failed him, too.

Bird Jaguar appeared shortly and Puuc left them. The king's face gave away nothing. In the dusty motes of sunlight, he could have been unreal, a spirit from another world. Even his voice seemed far away, disembodied.

"I have arranged to send you back."

"You haven't come to cut my throat?"

The king laughed. "You were very good out there. For one who has not played against a champion like Jeweled Skull, I was very proud."

Hugh was confused. "I—I failed. I must die."

"You will."

"But—"

"We defeated the Totil today. We won more games than they." His laughter boomed in the cavernous room. "One Shell finally defeated that braggart, Jeweled Skull. And I had the pleasure of sending him to *Xibalba* with my own hands. Ruby Snake has relinquished the lands he stole from me and he owes me much more in gold and slaves. I think that will be the end of his reign. We won't see him again."

"But, but—why did I not die?"

"You are my son. I reserve the right to kill you myself."

Hugh rose and gazed into the face of the king. He too, like Puuc, looked older, the creases in his face deeper, the eyes bleary, sad. But there was relief there also. "Chel-Te will earn his rightful inheritance after all," Hugh said. "I thought he would."

Bird Jaguar smiled. "I was surprised, shocked in fact, when the gods suddenly sent you to me. I didn't know what they were doing. But how could I not treat you as their messenger? My people needed a hero."

"And you gave them one."

A smile flickered across his lips. "Better than One Shell."

"Where is he?"

"He is a hero. He will escort the Totil back to their lands where he will become their governor. Of course, it suits my purpose to have him out of the way in a little, unimportant kingdom."

"Leaving you free to legitimize Chel-Te."

"As it should be. And you will be the last of the line of Lady Te-Xoc."

"Did you have to hit me so hard in the battle? I still feel the bruise."

Bird Jaguar took him by the shoulders and with a sudden movement hugged him to his chest. Brief. There were tears in his eyes.

A shadow hovered by the door.

"Come, Chel-Te," Hugh said, "unless you have come to kill me again."

The boy entered. He stood fiercely in the doorway. Gone was some of the timid uncertainty of a boy. He wore his newfound manhood like his royal mantle. Earlier, his father had wasted no time in publicly handing him his flapstaff, a staff of colorful ribbons and cloths, marking him as Malenche's legitimate heir.

"Aren't you afraid?" he asked.

Hugh shrugged. "I'll go back where I came from. My other kingdom."

"I—I wanted you to fail. I wanted you to die."

"Of course. You're Bird Jaguar's son."

The boy faltered. He held back his tears. "But you tried to save me, too. Do you not hate me?"

He shook his head. "You look fine in your new headdress. A king. Shield Jaguar Two, named after his grandfather."

Chel-Te pulled back his shoulders and raised his head proudly. "A son can have only one father."

The workmen had scarcely finished, for the quickly raised temple walls were still wet with plaster. Bird Jaguar pointed to the inscriptions on the lintel. "I hope you admire them."

Hugh nodded. On the sides of the doorway and the lintel above were carved the exploits of Blood Jaguar, son of Bird Jaguar, his arrival, his ascendancy, his famous battle in which he had defeated King Ruby Snake and Jeweled Skull. Of the ball game there was no mention.

"A fine legacy, Lord."

"No one will see it. Only you and I and the gods will know. I will have the temple buried tomorrow."

"The people should rightly see only Shield Jaguar Two, but I am satisfied."

"Then follow me."

"With your permission, Lord, leave me here a moment. Alone."

Bird Jaguar left him. Hugh bent to the bottom-most panel inscribed on the doorway. And in the dim torchlight, he inscribed in the wet plaster his own glyph.

He had entered Malenche from the depths of the pool. He would leave it that way also. Clad simply as he had been when he arrived in Malenche, in a loincloth and wearing gold ankle and wrist bracelets, he stood at the edge of the rock. Clenching his fingers to hold back the fear rising in him, he hoped desperately that the pool was a way back. If it wasn't...

A hushed silence descended upon the crowd who lined the area, while below him, the waters of the *cenote* were also calm and unruffled.

Bird Jaguar spoke loudly. "We have been honored by the gods who have sent us Blood Jaguar, yet it is our duty to return him to the place from where he came. As the sun nourishes us every day, so we will nourish him with his own son."

Puuc handed him the knife.

Bird Jaguar did not look at Hugh.

"Here is my well-beloved son," said Bird Jaguar.

"Here is my well-beloved father," Hugh replied.

A slight wind shifted among the flowing robes of the nobles. Hugh glanced up at the sky. The sun seemed to stop.

"Both will meet at the end of the world."

He saw the knife hover and bent his head.

It faltered. If Bird Jaguar refused, the world would end, the sun would die.

"Hu—!" There was a scream.

He felt the knife slide across his throat. Then a shoulder suddenly nudged him and he fell from the ledge through the air.

CHAPTER 12

"Hugh! Hugh!"

The sound was muffled, far away, ringing like a bell under water. He was dead wasn't he? Was this death? This deep sleep while being pulled in a slow drift toward the light?

"We're coming!"

A strong arm reached down and dragged him from the tugging vortex of the water. Hartmann Schele whipped his arm around his neck and pressed the point of the blade against his throat.

"Don't move," he commanded. "I won't hesitate to cut your throat—for real—you know that."

Hugh was fully alert now, his eyes wide with terror.

Schele turned his toward the figures coming down the slope. "Stop there, Falkins. Stop, or the boy will be killed."

Hugh's father, who had shouted for him, and Jose Morales, slid to a halt, sending a scatter of rocks down the slope. "What's going on here, Schele? Why are you dressed—my God! What are you doing to my son? Let him go!"

Schele laughed, his voice unnaturally loud. "The boy and I have unfinished business to discuss. Morales, throw your gun here! I know you have one."

"It's too late," Jose said. "We've got Garcia. We've got Ruiz too."

"Dad! Help me!" Hugh shouted again. He tried to twist out of the Schele's grasp but the man was too powerful.

"Where'd you get that scar on your neck, boy," Schele hissed.

"I fell on the rocks."

"Really." His voice was wheezing, mocking. "Look up at that platform above us. See it? Sacrificial victims were killed there by the high priests and sent to their deaths below, right where we are now. But," he paused, "I expect you know that already—Blood Jaguar."

"B-Blood Jaguar?" Hugh squirmed. "Man, have you flipped?"

"You are him. Don't deny it. Unless you die the *tun* will be repeated over and over. And I will never be king."

There was no point in denying the truth now. "Yes," he said.

"I should have killed you in the battle but that upstart king interfered. You should have died." His voice escalated to a scream.

He pulled Hugh to his feet and dragged him across a flat outcrop of rock.

"I'll finish what Bird Jaguar should have done." He raised the knife.

Hugh jabbed out with his feet, catching the man by surprise, knocking him to the ground, but Schele was up in an instant, slashing with the knife.

There was a flash and a roar.

Schele staggered back, blood spurting from his chest. His eyes glazed as he toppled in an awkward arc into the pool. He floundered, sputtering, his face contorted in pain and with a mighty effort he heaved himself onto the ledge. Miraculously, he still had the knife.

"Stop!" Jose Morales commanded.

Schele hugged the rock, taking in the figures of Jose and Roger Falkins standing above him. Then he turned his gaze back to Hugh.

"He'll send me away, H—Huu. Just like B-Bird Jaguar sent me away. I can't have that." The knife dropped into the water as his face contorted in pain. "I have to go. But I'll c-come back for you again."

He let go of the edge and fell back with a heavy splash. In a moment, the vortex of the pool grabbed him and sucked him under.

Hugh's father hugged him to his chest, tears flowing from his eyes. "What on earth were you trying to do, boy?" he said. "You scared me half to death when you disappeared again. Thank goodness Mitch had the sense to tell us where you were."

"And Schele?" Jose demanded. "What was that all about?"

Hugh took a deep breath. He explained about the sacrifice, suggesting that Schele was mentally unbalanced. But he left out the part about Malenche. His mind was still in a spin and he half believed that he had imagined it in his panic.

"Did he hurt you?" his father asked.

"No. I'm okay. Thanks for coming."

"Why are you dressed like that?"

"What was he shouting?"

"What about the guerrillas?"

"What about—"

"Stop!" Hugh pleaded. "My head's about to come off. One thing at a time."

They had returned to the camp as soon as possible after the encounter with Schele. All of the archaeologists had returned from the village, and when they saw him they began pumping him with questions. Again, he did not mention Malenche. He was also careful to skirt around the subject of the antiquities heist.

"I'm glad you're okay," Mitch said softly. "I was so worried."

He smiled back. "Hey. I didn't ask. What are all of you doing here? I thought the army kicked you out."

"Surprise coming up," David Kelly said.

The surprise was Jose Morales—Captain Jose Morales—of the Mexican National Army. He had returned the archaeologists to the camp, bringing with him a troop of very determined, professional-looking soldiers. He listened to Hugh's story intently, hand resting lightly on the gun strapped to his waist. He looked hard, efficient, not at all the laconic, easy-going archaeologist.

"We've been on Schele's and Garcia's tail for some time," he told them. "All we needed was proof of their complicity. So I disguised myself as an archaeologist to get some inside information. Schele seemed to disappear for long lengths of time, making me very suspicious. And the evacuation seemed rather odd, as *I* should have heard about it. So now we've hunted down most of Ruiz's men and captured Garcia as well. They won't be planning any raids for a long while."

Linda was furious. "I'm mad because I was tricked by those men. I didn't like them, but I never guessed what they were. You're a pretty good actor too."

He grinned. "I couldn't figure out why Schele was so disinterested in the well and the *midden*."

"He wanted you out of the area to get at the guns," Hugh said. "We must have walked right over them."

Jose thought hard. "Well that explains why there were so many accidents. Schele hoped to scare the whole team off the site. He hadn't counted on you getting in his way."

When the explaining was done, the group broke up to allow John Henry to examine Hugh's wounds, though not without his father hovering nearby. Henry's eyes widened in surprise. "Where have you been? Look at these cuts and bruises. Have you been in a fight?"

A flood of images roared through Hugh's mind, One Shell, the ball court, Jeweled Skull, the flash of the knife.

"I fell down the rocks," he said lamely. "That's all."

"You didn't get these falling down." Henry eyed him suspiciously. "Some of these are old cuts. This one on your neck was made with a dull knife. He pointed to Hugh's hand and arm. "And these bruises are old. What on earth…?"

Hugh's father suddenly grabbed Hugh's arm. He stared intently into his son's face, worry etched there but also surprise and shock. He whispered something to the doctor and John Henry nodded, leaving them alone.

"Falling down the rocks, indeed. I put off John Henry's suspicions but I know those cuts. They're sacrificial cuts. It was Schele who did this to you, wasn't it?" His face was hard a stone.

"You wouldn't believe me, Dad. No one would."

His father grinned. "I will. I know more than you think. So, tell me."

Hugh did.

Supper that night was a party. The archaeologists were in a fine mood, glad to be back on the site, glad that the "little war" hadn't done any serious damage. Jose promised to keep a close guard on the camp in case there were any further difficulties. He also planned a full-scale search of the ruins for more guns.

Mitch took Hugh aside. "The antiquities robbers still don't know we're onto them. They'll try to move that stuff tonight," she whispered. "We've got to stop them."

"How? What can we do?"

She thought hard. "Look, they can't move it all. They'd need some heavy equipment to do that. But they'll try to get the lighter, more valuable stuff out and hide it somewhere until the heat blows over. We'll find out where they've hidden it and watch who does it."

"Well…" Hugh hesitated.

Mitch overrode him. "No. I want to catch them myself. I owe it to you for suspecting your father anyway."

"Better let Jose handle it," Hugh suggested.

"Handle what?" Jose leaned nonchalantly against a tree. "I saw you two scheming away like mad at the camp. What are you up to? Isn't it a little late for…"

Mitch blushed. "We weren't—"

Hugh interrupted her quickly. "Mitch, Mitch. I think we could use a little help, don't you?"

Later that evening, he nestled in the notch where he had hidden before. Now the sounds of the night seemed comforting. Yet somewhere, hidden among the trees were Jose, Mitch and several soldiers.

"Someone's coming," Jose whispered from the darkness.

Hugh tensed himself, camera in hand.

There were five figures coming up the trail, the illumination from their flashlights bobbing ahead of them. They stopped by the door. "Only the best pieces," a man commanded. "And hurry. We've got a lot to do."

They entered the storeroom and minutes later came out with ceramic pots in their hands.

"We'll never get away with this. They're sure to find out," a woman complained.

"You're right," Hugh shouted. He stepped out from his refuge and snapped a picture as they turned in surprise. The woman screeched, dropping the pot she was carrying. It shattered with impact on the ground.

"Hold it right there!" Jose demanded. His soldiers slid out of the bush, surrounding them. Formally, he said, "Dr. Oliver Vasquez, Dr. Edith Richards, I arrest you in the name of the Mexican government. You and your helpers are charged with theft under the Antiquities Act."

Edith sagged against her co-conspirator. "Oh, no."

Vasquez sighed regretfully. "I should have known we might be spotted," he said. "We saw another set of footprints in the room and we chased someone, too. You?" he cocked his head at Mitch.

"Both of us, actually," she replied. "You gave us a good scare." She explained about the ghost-making machinery to Jose.

Edith sobbed. "We thought we'd frightened you away just like the workmen. You didn't come back."

Vasquez helped her to her feet. "Pull yourself together, woman."

"But I don't want to rot in a Mexican prison for the rest of my life. My career will be ruined."

"I'm surprised myself," Jose said bitterly. "You don't strike me as common thieves."

"We're not thieves," she said boldly. "We were trying to save some of the best pieces."

"From what?"

Vasquez answered for her, "From Sam Sheldon. That conniver sponsors a dig and waits until the last minute to pull the financial plug. Then he sends the archaeologists home leaving the place ripe for the taking. Everyone blames the local people for looting while he sells the best pieces on the black market."

Hugh remembered Sheldon's fine collections on his estate back in the U.S.A.

"Can you prove this?" Jose asked.

"No. It would be difficult. We had to take desperate measures."

Jose pondered the situation. "For now, you'll have to be under arrest. But send the workmen home with a stiff warning to keep their mouths shut or they'll answer to me."

Mitch took Hugh's hand as they headed back. "Will they get a tough sentence?"

He shook his head. "I think the police will let them off for taking in the big fish."

"Your father."

"Stepfather."

"Where will you go if Sheldon is caught? Back with your mother?"

He hesitated only a moment. "I want to stay here with my dad. If he'll have me."

Mitch chuckled. "Mine wants me to stay. He's afraid he'll lose me. But I've decided I want to get away. Maybe if I go to school and can get a 'real life.'"

"Will you go?"

"Yes. But not too soon. I've still got all summer." She put her arms around his neck and kissed him.

"Damn it, Roger," Joanne exploded. "Can't you hurry?"

Hugh was excited but anxious, too. He knew, of course, that archaeologists take a slow, painstaking, scientific approach to excavation, but when the tomb being excavated was the tomb of the mythic boy-king, Blood Jaguar…

"Yeah, c'mon."

"Break the seal, man."

"Just this once."

Hugh's father looked at his colleagues with a look of boyish mischief. "If your fellows at the university could hear you, they'd hang you by your degrees."

"I'm going to hang you by something else if you don't get on with it," Joanne promised.

"All right, everyone. I guess it isn't everyday this happens. And we deserve a bit of luck, too."

They were standing on the plaza the next day beside the circle of a small storage chamber—a *chultun* —that had been built over by an altar. The altar had been removed easily. In fact, it seemed to slide away as if its purpose were nothing more than the disguised cover for the *chultun*. All that remained was to break through the stone seal of the storage chamber.

"I just don't believe it," McVean said. "Here it was right under our feet all along. Roger, your instincts are incredible."

"Must be in the genes," Hugh's father corrected him. "It was my son, the archaeologist, who suggested to me that as Blood Jaguar might be a political compromise between Lady Xoc and Lady Eveningstar, they might bury him between the tombs of the two ladies."

They looked at Hugh with new respect.

"He's got the old man's knack, that's for sure," McVean said.

"The seal, Roger," Joanne complained.

"Yes. Yes, of course."

A few good blows of the sledgehammer were all that was needed. The plaster covering broke away and there was no lack of hands to help in excavating the rubble.

The storage chamber, as it turned out, was itself a disguise. Under the rubble they found a set of stairs.

"Just like Palenque," Linda breathed heavily. "I hope it doesn't take three years to dig, though."

It took less than three hours to open the stairway to the door of the tomb.

The honor of breaking the door went to Hugh. It was also a simple plaster affair designed to seal off the tomb rather than make it impregnable. He swung the sledgehammer and was gratified with a resounding echo. Poking his head inside to see, aided by a hissing kerosene lamp, he gasped.

"Whad'you see?"

Hugh remembered that when Henry Carter had been asked the same question upon breaking into the tomb of Tutankhamen, the boy-king of Egypt, he had replied "Wonders!" He called back nonchalantly, "Just some graffiti. Nothing much. Bird Jag Rules. Blud Jag wuz here."

"What?" his father shouted. "Let me in there."

The chamber was scarcely big enough for five of them to stand shoulder to shoulder where the light from the lamp did, indeed, show them wonders.

"Look, Roger." Joanne pointed at the relief carvings on the lintels. "It *is* Bird Jaguar."

Hugh's father could barely contain his excitement, like a young boy with a Christmas present. "Yes! Look, he's acknowledging Blood Jaguar as his son."

They all peered, one by one, to look at the object of their searches. Hugh smiled to himself. Bird Jaguar had been very clever. He had portrayed him, Blood Jaguar, as a Mayan, the same height as the others and with the same characteristic looks. And as if to further identify the warrior-king, they found a pot bearing the snarling likeness of a jaguar.

"Who's this?" Linda squealed, pointing at the carving of a woman. The woman was wearing a jade necklace.

Joanne translated. "The Lady Te-Xoc, mother of Blood Jaguar. From the line of Lady Xoc."

"That explains a lot," Hugh's father decided. "A political marriage of convenience."

"Could she be our *Lady*, do you think? Our unidentified skeleton?" Linda asked.

Hugh touched the carving gently, touched by the sadness of his remembrance.

Their lights glinted off gold. Dazzling gold. Gold piled from floor to ceiling. Everything from pots to pendants, the storeroom was filled to capacity with hundreds of pieces of art. They could only stare at it in hushed wonder.

"Hey. Our turn," David Kelly called from the outside. "And we've also got a visitor."

They emerged from the tomb to greet Don Alfonso. The old man formally acknowledged Hugh's father but deliberately, Hugh noticed, avoided eye contact with him.

It was Puuc. They knew, both of them.

The old man was shown around the tomb as if he himself was a royal visitor and Don Alfonso seemed pleased with the discovery. He had also come to conduct the ceremony, the *hetzmek* of Hugh Falkins.

After supper, when the excitement of the discovery had subsided, they arranged themselves around the table. The ceremony was usually for babies but the old man explained that older youth could also have one to celebrate a new phase of life. Several objects lay on the table: a book, an archaeologist's trowel, a piece of string, a weeding blade—and several more.

The old man nodded sagely as he spoke. "*Koten, Hugh Falkins, ten kin mentik hetzmek tech.* Come, Hugh Falkins, I make the *hetzmek* for you. Here are all the things I give to you to grasp. You need them to become a man."

He paused dramatically, his gaze fixed firmly on Hugh now, sharing their secret.

"I give you the book that you may read, the trowel that you may discover, the string that you may tie yourself to someone in marriage, a weeding blade that you may tend your father's farm…"

Hugh was a bit confused by some of it but he understood that the objects were the things he would use later in life. Each of his friends had also placed an object on the table that he or she wished for Hugh's good luck. One of them was a Team Yax T-shirt, which he wore proudly.

Finally, Don Alfonso took him astride his hip, a difficult and amusing thing to do since they were nearly two feet apart in height. It was symbolic of the mother who took the new baby on her hip to signify his passage from infancy to babyhood. Hugh, it was made to understand, had made the passage from boy to man. They circled counterclockwise nine times around the table and Don Alfonso wrapped him in a blanket to protect his inner soul.

"Usually," Don Alfonso grinned, "the children are dismissed after this and the parents celebrate with much feasting and drinking of *balche*, fermented corn."

"And I give you this, Hugh Falkins," Mitch intoned in her best Don Alfonso voice, walking forward to Hugh with an enormous birthday cake glowing with candles, "that you make pig of yourself. Happy *Hetzmek*."

Everyone clapped and made their way through the cake faster than breaking into Blood Jaguar's tomb. Even Don Alfonso attacked the cake with energy. "*Mucho gusto*," he beamed. And afterward, there was indeed much drinking of *balche*.

"I knew you were in trouble, even without Mitch's help," his father said to Hugh. "I just had this sixth sense—or a bad dream. I imagined that a jaguar told me something was wrong."

"You were just in time," Hugh said with relief. "I'm glad you can sense things."

His father regarded him seriously. "The spirit world can be dangerous, Hugh. I can only see and hear them. But you have the power to go among them. You must be very careful. It's not a power to be abused or taken lightly."

He paused to light his pipe. "Your mother was afraid. She feared the world she couldn't see or touch. It was unnerving to her."

They remained silent and watched the blue smoke rise into the air.

His father sighed. "In the end, it was just too much for her." A smile flitted across his face. "Of course, she knows nothing about your more dangerous escapades. She's happy and that's all I want for her. Do you understand?"

Hugh didn't think he really expected an answer. "It would be incredible to go back into time when you wanted, wouldn't it?"

"You can if you want."

"How?"

His father gripped his son's shoulder. "I need another good archaeologist. Even if it means delving into the past the traditional way."

"Do you mean it? What about mom?"

"I think we can get over that hurdle," he said. "I talked to her and she's agreeable as long as," he chuckled, "as long as you're safe. Sheldon phoned earlier, too. He's a worried man. He'll continue to sponsor the project and I think he understands that he's under investigation. So I don't expect trouble from him, either."

"Then I'd like to stay."

He heard the cough of the jaguar.

"Ah," he said, "there you are. Thank you for everything."

The jaguar stood in the middle of the trail, its coal-red eyes fixed on his, its tail swinging languidly. It grunted again, turned away, then looked back at Hugh once more. Hugh thought it smiled. Then it was gone into the darkness.

He continued his walk down to the plaza, aided by a single flashlight. As there was no further need for a guard, he walked to the tomb of Blood Jaguar without being stopped.

There was still a lingering doubt in his mind.

He descended the stairs and through the enlarged hole, covered by a tarpaulin. In the chamber, the light flickered off the familiar faces of Bird Jaguar, Lady Eveningstar, Chel-Te and his mother, Te-Xoc. He touched the stone carving with affection, and their eyes watched him with interest.

He ignored the gold and went to the foot of the inner wall where a panel of glyphs had been inscribed. Squatting near them, he played the light over them, his heart beating rapidly.

He had to know for sure.

The light fixed on the last glyph, crudely drawn in the plaster, where it had been undisturbed for over one thousand years.

He recognized it at once. The glyph showed a hooded beak, rounded head and gleaming eye. His glyph.

The falcon.

ABOUT THE AUTHOR

Allan Serafino lives in Calgary, Alberta, with his wife, Maureen. For many years he was a schoolteacher before he entered a long career as a non-profit agency manager. He travels extensively around the world, which has given him ideas for many more Hugh Falkins mysteries. He has published two books of poetry and is now hard at work on an adventure novel about climbing in the Rocky Mountains near his home.

About *Blood Jaguar* he says, "The idea for the book came while studying archaeology in Mexico. While I was alone inside a dark Mayan temple I began to hear mysterious 'voices,' almost as if the ancient Mayans carved on the stone walls were calling to me. It was incredibly spooky. What if they were here? What if I had traveled to the past? From that moment the story was born."

MORE GREAT KIDS' FICTION FROM LTDBOOKS...

Lou Dunlop: Private Eye
By Glen Ebisch

Available in Trade Paperback and eBook formats !

Lou is an average high school kid with average problems—until one of the students in his class disappears. When an outrageous blonde named Jessie convinces Lou to search for the missing girl, he gets more excitement than he ever expected.

The Right Hand of Velachaz
By Rie Sheridan

Available in eBook formats!

Twelve-year-old Teman finds himself drawn into a world he never dreamed he'd be a part of—a world of magic and dragons. Plucked from the streets to help the wizard Velachaz hide a secret past, Teman soon discovers that he shares the gift of Magic. When he meets the wizard's nephew Galen, a strange young knight who is off to slay a dragon, the quest is on!

Visit www.LTDBooks for more information
on our more than 100 titles!